Worship

Book Two
in the
H3RO Series

An Atlantis Entertainment Novel

J. S. Lee

Axellia
Publishing

Axellia Publishing

First Edition, December 2018
Published by Axellia Publishing

Print ISBN: 978-1-912644-16-2
eBook ASIN: B07K5VBV7W

Cover design by Natasha Snow Designs;
www.natashasnowdesigns.com

Edited by C. Lesley
Proofread by S. Harvell

CONTENTS

DEDICATION

For my girls, Sarah and Leanne

And my boys, Monsta X

THE ATLANTIS ENTERTAINMENT UNIVERSE

Reverse Harem
(As J. S. Lee)

H3RO

Idol Thoughts
Idol Worship
Idol Gossip

Onyx

ONYX: Truth
ONYX: Heart
ONYX: Love
ONYX: Unity
ONYX: Forever

Young Adult Contemporary Romance
(As Ji Soo Lee)

Zodiac

The Idol Who Became Her World
The Girl Who Gave Him The Moon
The Dancer Who Saved Her Soul
The Leader Who Fell From The Sky

Coming Soon

The Boy Who Showed Her The Stars

Serenity Ackles & J. S. Lee
Urban Fantasy Reverse Harem

The Goddess of Fate & Destiny

Cursed Luck
Stolen Luck

Coming Soon

Twisted Luck
Chosen Luck

K-101

For those of you unfamiliar with K-Pop / K-Dramas / Korean culture, here's a short handy guide:

Names

Names in Korean are written family name then given name. It's not uncommon to use the full name when addressing a person—even one you're close to.

박현태 is the Korean way of writing Park Hyuntae (Tae). Tae is pronounced like Tay.

권민혁 is the Korean way of writing Kwon Minhyuk

하균구 is the Korean way of writing Ha Kyungu (Kyun)

송준기 is the Korean way of writing Song Junki (Jun)

Nate and Dante are a little different as they are American-Korean and Chinese. Nate isn't a Korean name and would therefore be spelled out phonetically in Korean. The same for Dante. (For those curious, it would be 네이트 for Nate, and 단테 for Dante.)

Surnames (Family names)

As the western worlds combined, we ended up with a lot of variation in surnames. In Korea, although there is variation, you will find a lot Kims, Lees, and Parks. To try to keep things as easy to follow as possible, I have tried to make sure that all characters don't have the same surname *unless* they're in the same family—like Holly. However, in reality, this is most often not the case.

BTS, for example have Kim Namjoon (RM), Kim Seokjin (Jin), and Kim Taehyung (V). They all share the same family name, but are not related.

Oppa (오빠), hyung (형), noona (누나), and oennie (언니)

This one gets a little confusing at first. The first thing you need to know, in Korea, age is a very important thing. It's not uncommon for you to be asked your age before your name because you need to be spoken to with the correct level of respect (known as honorifics). To show this, there's actually several ways to speak to address a person and it usually depends on your age (an exception to this might be in a place of work where someone younger than you is more senior to you). But I'll keep this simple and limit to myself to terms used in the book.

Traditionally, oppa, hyung, noona, and unnie are terms used to describe your older sibling—depending on what sex you are and what sex they are. If you are male, your older brother is hyung and your older sister is noona. If you are female, your older brother is your oppa, and your older sister is unnie (technically, 언니 when Romanized is oenni, but unnie has become a more standard way of writing this). However, this can often be transferred to people you are close to. A girl will call her older boyfriend oppa. An idol will call his older groupmates hyung.

Sunbae (선배) and Hoobae (후배)

Along the same vein, sunbae (senior) and hoobae (junior) may be used as an alternative when using experience as a basis, rather than age.

Other

Comeback: this is an odd one for most people. Your next single isn't just your next single. It's a comeback—and it doesn't matter if you've waited two months or two years.

Kakao: Kakao is a messaging app similar to Whatsapp or Wechat.

SNS: What we would call Social Media, Koreans use the term Social Networking Service. Included in this would be **V Live**, an app which allows Korean idols to communicate with their fans (a bit like Instagram Live)

화이팅: Fighting, or 'hwaiting' is a word commonly used as encouragement, like 'good luck' or 'let's do this'.

Maknae: a term used for the youngest member of a group.

'Ya!': The Korean equivalent to 'Hey!'

제 X 장: Chapter (pronounced jae X jang)

Character Bios are also available at the back of this book

More terms and information is available on Ji Soo's website: www.jislooleeauthor.com/k101

제1 장

H3R으

Tell Them

The drive back to the dorm from the Inkigayo performance was like torture for me. Despite the numerous text messages from Lee Sejin—*now* he wanted to see me—I wasn't going to hurry the guys. They may not have gotten the Inkigayo win, but they were still thrilled about the Gaon win. They had held their heads high as the winners reperformed their song, and then stuck around to congratulate the other groups. They'd even received their own selection of compliments and I wasn't going to do anything to wipe the smiles from their faces.

Not tonight.

My face was actually hurting from the smile I'd fixed on it.

"Noona, you promised us meat!" Jun, H3RO's maknae, called from the back of the minibus. He was still bouncing around in excitement.

"I know I did," I responded, keeping the smile on my face. "But you guys need a shower and to get all that makeup off. Go battle over the bathroom, and I will take us out later." They all bounded out of the minibus and disappeared upstairs, chatting animatedly.

Finally alone, I let the smile fall from my face. Feeling like a prisoner walking the green mile, I trudged to the Atlantis Entertainment building and went straight up to Sejin's office. I was about to go in when Tae appeared beside me. "Why are you here?" he asked, confused.

"You should head back to the dorm," I instructed him, ignoring his question. "You need to get that makeup off and cleanse your face."

He was still wearing what he'd performed in, from the eyeliner, right down to all his performance clothes, complete with various pieces of jewelry. "Why are you here?" he asked again.

"I have a meeting with Lee Sejin," I shrugged. "Don't worry about it. You go back and enjoy what is left of the afternoon."

"You're acting strange," he said. Tae's eyes were usually serious and intense, and right now they were eyeing me with a deep curiosity.

The door opened and Sejin was standing there, glowering at me. "How much longer do you plan on making us wait?" he demanded. He then turned his attention to Tae, arching an eyebrow in amusement. "And we have H3RO's leader too? You might as well come in and join us as you're here."

"That's not necessary," I objected, hurriedly.

Tae shot me a questioning look, but stepped past Sejin into his office.

"Please don't do this in front of him," I quietly begged Sejin.

He ignored me and marched into his office, joining his father on one of the hideous leather couches.

He pointed to the one opposite. Tae sat as requested, bowing his head respectfully at the Chairman and Vice Chairman. I sat down beside him, but only because my legs had turned to jelly and I had about four more seconds before they gave out on me.

"You got a number one," Sejin announced.

Tae nodded. "Yes, sir. The Gaon Singles Chart. It was largely thanks to Holly."

"But it's only one number one," he continued.

"Their first number one!" I cried. "And it could have been two or more if the physical copies of the albums had been distributed on time."

"And did my sister explain to you what would happen if you only got one number one?" Sejin pressed, ignoring me.

Tae frowned, looking from Sejin to myself, then back at Sejin. "Your sister?"

Sejin pointed at me. "Holly. Didn't she tell you?"

I dropped my head, unable to look at Tae. I had intentionally hidden the fact that Lee Sejin was my half-brother, and that I was the illegitimate daughter of owner and founder of Atlantis Entertainment, Lee Woojin.

Unless you knew this information, you wouldn't be able to tell from looking. Sejin looked very much like his father—tall and lanky, with a long face whereas I took after my mother with her short height, double eyelids and pointed chin.

I could feel the energy surrounding Tae change, and not just because he moved away from me. "What would happen with a number one single?" he asked, carefully. I could feel his eyes burning into the side of my head.

"I was going to disband H3RO," Sejin explained, like the idea of disbanding them was as ordinary a decision as picking a side dish. "But I told her, that if you guys could get a number one on your comeback, I would let you guys keep your contracts."

"Then that's a good thing," Tae responded, slowly. Carefully.

"If it were only that simple," Sejin tutted. "Holly decided one wasn't a big enough challenge and promised two."

"It wasn't like that!" I cried, finally turning to look at Tae. I wished I hadn't when all I saw was betrayal there. I turned to Sejin. "And we could have done it if we'd have had those album sales."

"H3RO didn't even rank in the top three on Inkigayo," Sejin told me, coldly. "Physical copies or not, they wouldn't have hit the Inkigayo number one, nor the Gaon Album chart."

"We got a number one!" I cried, pleading with him. "You can't disband them off the back of that!"

"You've already made the decision for me," Sejin shrugged, although he looked smug with himself.

I couldn't stop the tears leaking from my eyes. I also couldn't bring myself to look at H3RO's leader. But Tae deserved better than that, so I forced myself to face him. "I'm sorry," I told him, barely able to see him through the tears. Tae's stare had turned cold and foreign. It was like I no longer knew the person staring back at me, and I couldn't blame him. "I'm sorry," I said again, reaching out for him.

Tae jerked out of the way, getting to his feet. "I'd best tell the others." His voice was unrecognizable too. Upset, hurt, disappointed.

Fuck it.

I had nothing to lose.

I dropped to my knees in front of Sejin. "Please," I begged him. "Please do not punish H3RO because of my failure. Please. I'll go back to America if you want me to, but please, please don't disband H3RO." I dropped my head into a kowtow. There was no shame anymore. I was prepared to do anything I needed to, to keep them together. "*Please.*" At Sejin's feet, the only thing left for me to do was pray.

So, I did.

Then my miracle happened.

"Did anyone specify when this second number one was supposed to occur?" I looked up at Lee Woojin who had spoken, but didn't dare breathe, let alone say anything.

Sejin pulled a face. "Well, no, but—"

"There were no timelines agreed?" he pressed.

"No!" I suddenly cried.

Sejin shot me a murderous look. "We were discussing this comeback," he said, derisively.

Woojin shrugged, looking between us both. "But, to be clear, there was nothing to specify that *this* comeback was required to have two number ones?"

"Technically, no," Sejin whined, suddenly acting like he was a six-year-old. "But it was implied."

"As far as I see it, if the terms were not clearly specified, then the disbandment cannot be based upon this single number one. However, as a second number one was mentioned, I fully expect that the next comeback will have one."

I blinked up at him, trying to see my father through my tears. "Huh?"

"H3RO have survived this comeback. The next one is up to you."

I stared up at him, unable to move, sure that if I did, I was either going to faint or cry. Neither of which was appealing.

Then, behind me, a door slammed shut.

I turned. Tae had gone.

Tae!

I got to my feet and nodded my head at Lee Woojin. "Thank you," I told him, sincerely. And then I ran from the room, trying to find Tae.

He must have only had a few seconds head start, but he was nowhere in sight. I ran down the corridor to the elevator—there was one going down. Hammering on the call button wasn't getting the other one to appear any time soon, but we were thirty-five floors up and running down the stairs was beyond my fitness level.

It took an age for the elevator to appear, and by the time I got outside, if Tae had been ahead of me, he had a huge head start on me. For half a moment, I contemplated going back to the apartment Lee Woojin had gotten for me, rather than the dorm, and hiding away from my problems, but I wasn't that type of girl.

Instead, I returned into Atlantis to use the restroom and make sure my face wasn't a complete wreck from all the crying. I didn't want them to find out this way, but I didn't regret my decision not to tell them. I was certain that would have caused more problems and their album would never have turned out so well otherwise.

Running a hand through my hair one last time, I left the safety of the restroom and made the short walk back to the dorm.

My hand hovered over the door's lock, waiting for me to type in the access code, but I couldn't do it. I'd spent the short trip back trying to work out what to say, or rather, how to say it, and I was still coming up short. I brought my hand back, balling it up into a fist, then let out a long sigh. Instead, I retreated back into the elevator and went up to the roof.

The dorms, like most buildings in Seoul, had access to the rooftop. Although it was missing grass, there were potted plants everywhere and in the center, just behind the door, was a small sheltered area. It was a place I had been using as a second office, preferring the fresh air to the confines of the room at Atlantis Entertainment. It had a suite of outdoor furniture, and as it was one of the higher buildings, wasn't overlooked.

I started towards it, then stopped as flashes of my night with Nate entered my head. It had been up here on the roof, on one of those couches, that Nate and I had slept with each other. I closed my eyes, briefly reliving the touch of his hands and lips on my body. The memory sent warm fuzzies dancing over my skin, almost as though I could feel his touch once more.

Then Tae's betrayed face popped into my mind.

I bypassed the seated area, moving over to the edge of the building. The dorm, and the office, were both on the south side of the river in Gangnam. If you found the right part of the rooftop and looked through the other buildings, you could just catch a glimmer of the Han River.

I didn't look. Instead, I hung my head with a sigh, resting my elbows on the edge of the building. I didn't doubt that Tae was in there, telling the other five members of H3RO who I was.

It was stupid. I had a messed-up relationship with Lee Woojin. OK, relationship was a generous term for the man I hadn't known had existed until ten months ago when he demanded I move to Seoul to work in his company. Until then, my 'father' was just a man in my mom's past. Why would I tell them?

I kicked at the concrete wall. I didn't because I didn't want them to think I was there to disband them. They—Kyun, in particular—had been suspicious of that. The reason I was up here now wasn't because I was trying to work out what to tell them. Not really … I was up here because I didn't want to see the looks of betrayal on their faces.

It had been bad enough when I had seen it on Tae.

I sucked in a deep breath. It was late summer and the air was already hot and humid. We could have done with that a few weeks ago when we were filming in the cold and rain. However, it meant that it wasn't quite the fresh air that I needed.

I blew the breath out slowly, and then turned, letting out a squeal of fright at Tae's disappointed face being right in front of me. "Tae!"

His arms were folded and he was eyeing me warily, like I was a puppy that had bitten him once and he wasn't sure if I was going to do it again. "I would ask if it's all true, but I don't see why Lee Sejin would make that up."

I nodded, chewing at me lip. Finally, I wrapped my arms around myself, rubbing at a chill which had set in, despite the warm air. "Lee Woojin is my father on paper only," I told him.

"The same paper H3RO's contracts are written

on," Tae responded. His tone was eerily calm.

"There has not been one part of this comeback where I have ever considered or wanted to disband H3RO," I told him, firmly. "I will admit that when I told Sejin I would see to it H3RO would get two number ones that I didn't understand exactly what that would mean, nor did I realize just how much Atlantis was working against that happening, but here we are with a number one single, and I will continue to do everything in my power to make sure you guys get a second one."

"How could you not tell us?" he asked, simply.

I chewed at my lip again, before shrugging. "You were all convinced that I was here to disband you. If you knew who I was, I wasn't sure you would trust me."

"I'm not sure I trust you now," Tae responded. His voice had gone blunt, but the words were sharp enough to make me wince.

"Have you told the others?"

Tae slowly shook his head. "I wanted to, but I thought it was something that should come from you. I might not have been afforded that luxury, but they can be."

"Where …" I cleared my throat, finding it thick and hard to get the words out. "Where does that leave us?"

"Honestly, I don't know," he admitted. "I see why you did it, but I am really pissed off with you right now. I'm not sure I want to be around you."

A lump formed in my throat, and I fought to keep the tears back as I nodded. "I'm going to tell them now," I said. I didn't wait for him, hurrying over to the door. He joined me in the elevator but didn't say a word, avoiding my eyes in the metallic reflection.

Inside the dorm, I found the other five members of H3RO waiting for me. I had forgotten that I had promised them barbeque. "About time," Jun grumbled, although he was rubbing his stomach good naturedly. "I thought I was going to die of starvation."

"Or you could have made some ramyun to tide you over," Minhyuk said, rolling his eyes.

"I could, but Holly promised meat. I want to make sure I can eat as much as possible!"

I moved over in front of the television. "You guys should sit."

"Are we being disbanded?" Kyun instantly asked.

I sighed wearily. "Just sit."

Nate walked over to me, placing a hand on each shoulder to peer down at me. "Is everything OK?"

I side stepped from his grasp with another sigh. "There's something I need to tell you all," I said, quietly. I chewed at my lip, trying to remember what I'd silently rehearsed. "My mom is from outside of Daegu, originally. In the country, in fact. She met my father, fell in love, and fell pregnant with me. When she told him, he basically chased her from South Korea. She went to Chicago where she had me."

"Holly?" Nate questioned from beside me.

"I had no idea who he was until he turned up last year, insisting that I move back here and take my place in the family business," I pressed on, ignoring the look Nate was giving me. He knew. He had from almost the beginning. He wasn't the only one: I glanced over at Jun, to find him studying me with his head cocked. "My father is Lee Woojin."

"Lee Woojin?" Dante repeated.

Kyun's eyes narrowed. "You mean the Chairman of Atlantis Entertainment, Lee Woojin?"

I nodded.

"So, you *are* here to disband us!"

"*Hyung!*" Jun exclaimed. "Do you really think Holly would have worked so hard on our comeback if she wanted to disband us?"

"But she's one of them," he snapped, angrily.

"Not by choice," I told him. "Trust me, I was perfectly happy not knowing who my father was, or that I was the half-sister of that asshole," I added, unable to keep the scorn from my voice.

"They have lied to us for years," Kyun scoffed. "Which is what you've been doing since the beginning. How are you any different?"

I hung my head. He wasn't wrong, and I had no response to that.

"Yet she's been fighting for us since the beginning," Nate pointed out. He stepped closer, his hand resting on the small of my back.

I drew strength from it, knowing there was at least one person in this room who wasn't going to hate me at the end of this conversation. I sucked in a deep breath. "Lee Sejin wanted to disband you, yes," I continued. "I didn't. I never did. In fact, I was that confident in you guys, that I made a stupid agreement with him."

"What?" Minhyuk asked. I finally looked at the beanpole thin member of H3RO. He was gazing back at me with confusion, but his look was missing the betrayal that was still clear in Tae from behind him, and the complete distrust that was in Kyun's.

"He said that in order to keep from ending your contracts, H3RO needed to get a number one."

Minhyuk shrugged. "We did that," he pointed out, then grinned. "'Who Is Your Hero?' got to number one!"

"What was the agreement?" Kyun demanded.

"That I would get you two," I admitted.

"So, we are being disbanded?" he cried, his words sounding choked up.

"Not yet," Tae said, stepping forward to wrap an arm around Kyun's shoulders. "Lee Woojin said Holly and Lee Sejin had never specified what the terms were clearly."

"But we're not safe yet?" Kyun asked, looking at his friend.

Tae slowly shook his head. "Not yet, but we did it once. We can do it again."

Kyun shook himself free of Tae's grasp, then stormed off down the hallway. Seconds later, the door to his bedroom slammed closed behind him. Tae shot me a pointed look, then followed after Kyun.

I stared after them, trying not to cry. Then my view was blocked by Dante, the t-shirt he was wearing doing nothing to hide the exceedingly defined torso of his. I looked up, just as he wrapped his arms around me, pulling me into a tight bearhug.

"You can't keep shit like this from us," he chided me, gently. "Even if your brother is an asshole."

"Half-brother," I corrected him, my voice muffled thanks to his chest.

He gave me a squeeze, then stepped back. "Kyun is …" he frowned. "He worries a lot. It might take a while, but he's going to see what we do."

"What?" I asked, peering up at him with curiosity.

"That you're H3RO's hero!" Jun exclaimed.

The house had a large drive with a fountain in the middle of it. However, instead of a traditional feature, it was sporting a statue of a trident in it, matching the Atlantis Entertainment logo. I really had to fight with myself not to roll my eyes at that.

The single-story house looked traditional, but looking at the brickwork, I had a feeling this was a new build designed to look much older than it was. I also had a suspicion it was like the TARDIS—much bigger on the inside than it looked from out front.

I parked up and made my way to the door. Like the gate, it opened before I could knock. A man in a suit stood waiting. "Please come in," he requested, bowing at me.

I did as he said, following him into a grand entrance hall. Lined with plants, and another water feature in the center (this one with koi in the raised pond), if anyone had any doubts as to how rich my father was, they would be quashed at this.

The butler led me further into the house, down long hallways which had various pieces of art adorning them. Instead of feeling lucky that I was part of this family, it just made me angry. My mom had struggled financially when I was growing up. It wasn't until my early teens that she had scraped together enough money to buy the small restaurant she still owned, and it turned over enough that she could help me with my student loans.

I'd never felt hard done by, but I knew how hard my mom had worked. Meanwhile, Lee Woojin was over here, living the life of luxury. I knew enough to know that he hadn't grown up poor either.

I was led into a large dining room at the back of

the house, where, like his office, the walls were fifty percent glass. The sun was streaming in, brightening the room, but the temperature was kept at a pleasant level.

Already seated at the table was Lee Woojin, a woman who was probably my grandmother, Lee Sejin, and a younger male. He was my youngest brother, Seungjin.

"You're late," my grandmother snapped, irritably.

I refrained from looking at my watch, knowing full well I had arrived half an hour earlier than requested. According to my mom, she was the reason she had been *persuaded* to leave for Chicago. Clearly, she didn't like the idea of me being here.

Apparently, this wasn't a meeting regarding H3RO. I was half-tempted to leave, but instead, I took the only free seat, opposite her, next to Seungjin, in silence. I stared at her, keeping my expression blank.

"This is your grandmother." Lee Woojin started to introduce her, but she cut him off.

"You will call me Park Sonha," she informed me.

"I'd like to call you something else," I muttered under my breath, in English.

"I beg your pardon?"

I fixed her a pleasant smile as I set a pure white napkin in my lap. "It's a pleasure to meet you after all these years," I told her politely. "My mother speaks so fondly of you."

"Your mother was a gold digger," Park Sonha snapped.

"*Eomeoni*!" Lee Woojin admonished. I'll admit, that surprised me.

"It runs in the family," Lee Sejin muttered, loud enough to be heard.

I closed my eyes and counted to ten. It didn't work: I was still seething. Instead, I pulled the napkin from my lap and deposited it on the table as I stood. "Well, this was worth getting out of bed for," I announced. Then I left, ignoring Lee Woojin's protests. What did he expect? That I was going to sit there and listen to his mother insult mine? The hell with that.

Unfortunately, I got lost on the way back to the front door.

I hadn't been paying that much attention to the direction I was going, but more the wealth that oozed out of the walls. Now I had no idea where I was. So much for a smooth getaway.

Thankfully, I found the door, but when I stepped outside, I also found someone waiting for me, leaning against the driver's door of my Range Rover. "Hi," Seungjin greeted me, warily.

I stared at him, just as warily. This was the first conversation we'd ever had. He was six years younger than me, and a whole fourteen years younger than his older brother, Sejin. "Hello," I returned, slowly.

"Do you want to go somewhere a little less uncomfortable for some breakfast? There's a place near the dorms which serves really good porridge?"

He, like Sejin, was tall. They must have gotten the height genes from our father, because I certainly hadn't. I realized he was waiting patiently for a response, and I quickly nodded, unlocking the car.

We drove in silence back to the dorm, where I left the car, then we walked, still in silence, to the place he was referring to. Seungjin had pulled on a cap and a mask and kept his head down as we walked over. I didn't know the full details, but I did know the group he was in, Bright Boys, had been caught up in some scandal and he was trying to keep a low profile.

The restaurant was run by a lovely middle-aged woman who seemed to know Seungjin, offering him a table in the back, out of the way. We managed to get the bowls of porridge in front of us without saying anything other than our order. I sighed. "I'm sorry I've not spoken to you before now," I told him. "I don't have the greatest relationship with Sejin and I wasn't sure if you would want to meet with me either."

"I got your message from Youngbin," Seungjin told me. "I contemplated calling you a few times."

I nodded. I had asked Youngbin, leader of another group at Atlantis, Onyx, to pass on my number to Seungjin. If Seungjin wanted to meet me, I wanted it to be on his terms.

"I thought you'd be like them."

"Them?" I questioned.

"They don't like the fact I'm an idol. I think they're happy that things are going wrong with Bright Boys because they want to disband us too," he muttered, glumly, stirring his porridge around.

"I'm sure that's not the case," I told him.

He looked up at me with solemn eyes. "Which bit?"

I set my spoon down. "Seungjin, I am not here to get in the middle of things with you and your family."

"We're your family too," he pointed out. "And I don't want you to get in the middle of things, but you've saved H3RO. Can't you save us too?"

I hadn't completely saved H3RO yet, but I didn't want to tell him that. "I'm H3RO's manager, not Bright Boys," I informed him.

"But father is trying to get you to take a senior position at Atlantis, so you'll be able to do something there, right?" he asked desperately.

"If I didn't know any better, I'd think you were making moves on my girl," a familiar voice announced.

I had never been so grateful to see Jun.

Seungjin looked up at him and pulled a face. "Gross. She's old."

Jun clipped him around the back of the head. As the one who was usually being chided or smacked in H3RO, I could tell he enjoyed that. "Ya!" He took the seat next to me and pulled my half-eaten bowl of porridge towards him.

I reached for my spoon and used it to smack the back of his hand. "I don't think so, mister." I pulled the bowl back. "And come on, you know he's my brother."

Jun pouted at me. "Noona, I'm hungry!"

"Oh, have it, I'm full anyway," I muttered, pushing the bowl back. I looked to Seungjin. "Look, I don't know what's happening with Bright Boys, but for now, just keep your head down."

"She's right," Jun agreed, mouth full of food. "Keep out of the spotlight for a bit."

I turned to Jun with a frown. "Why are you here?"

He pointed at the bowl. "I was hungry."

Seungjin's phone bleeped and he pulled it out to read a message. "I have to go. Do you like bowling?" I nodded. "Want to do that; next time?"

I settled back, resting my hands in my lap. "Sure," I agreed, watching him leave. For a first meeting, I wasn't sure how that went, seeing as he seemed to want to speak about Bright Boys, but if he wanted to hang out again, maybe not as bad as I thought?

I jumped when Jun's hand took one of mine, resting them on my lap under the table. "Are you OK?" he asked me.

I stared down at his hand, before looking up at him. I nodded. "I'm fine," I sighed.

"I haven't seen much of you since you told everyone about your family."

"You mean since last night," I told him, pulling a face. "I've only been gone a few hours."

"Still missed you," he shrugged.

"Missed me? Or missed the fact we didn't go out for barbeque last night?" I asked, fighting back a smile. When all was said and done last night, no one had felt like going out.

"Can't it be both?" He leaned an elbow on the table, propping his head up as he tried to give me wide puppy dog eyes.

I couldn't stop the giggle. "Really?" I asked, as he batted his eyes at me. "Pabo." *Fool.* I tugged my hand free and stood. "If everyone feels up to it, we can go out tonight. It's only Dante who has to be up early tomorrow, and I think you all deserve it."

We left the restaurant and started the short walk back to the dorm. Halfway back, Jun slipped his hand into mine, tugging me back to him. "I was serious before," he said.

"So was I," I shrugged. "We can get food later."

Jun's hand left mine, then both settled on my hips. "I missed you."

My heart started pounding in my chest as he stared down at me. I brought my hands up, settling them just above Jun's elbows as I stared back up at him. In the back of my mind, a small voice was trying hard to be heard—*you slept with Nate!*—but the rest of my mind was trying to block it. I was attracted to Jun, but not only that, he, like Nate, had also known who I was and not been upset by it …

His thumbs started moving up and down over my hips, and I closed my eyes, enjoying his touch, waiting for his kiss. Instead, I was brought back to reality by a smack to my head.

Literally.

Something hit the back of my head so hard, not only did I scream in shock, my head jerked forward, headbutting Jun.

"LEAVE SONG JUNKI ALONE!" someone screamed.

One hand shot up to my forehead, while the other went to the back of my head, trying to work out what was going on, and what hurt more. When the fingers on the back of my head touched wet, I panicked. "I'm bleeding!" I cried.

"Holly?" Jun questioned in alarm. He reached up for my head.

I winced as he gently prodded it, then my eyes went wide. "You're bleeding!" I exclaimed, as blood trickled from his nose.

"You're not," he assured me, wiping the blood from his nose with back of his other hand. "It's an egg."

"I TOLD YOU TO LEAVE SONG JUNKI ALONE!" a voice screamed again, before another egg exploded against the wall next to me.

"She's my manager!" Jun yelled back.

I turned, trying to see where the voice was coming from, but all I could see was a woman in a cap running away. I took a step after her, but Jun's hand shot around my wrist and he started pulling me back to the dorm. "Jun, we need to catch her."

"She's gone," he disagreed. "We need to make sure you're OK."

"I'm not the one bleeding," I pointed out.

"Just come with me," he ordered, leading me inside and to the elevator.

제3 장

H3RO

Hot Boy

Inside, I peered up at Jun's nose, pulling a Kleenex from my purse. "I'm sorry," I muttered, dabbing at his nose.

"Why are you apologizing?" he asked, taking the tissue from me.

"Because I headbutted you," I shrugged.

The elevator pinged open and we walked into the apartment. Minhyuk was in there, busy baking something. He glanced up at us, returned his attention to measuring out some sugar, and then did a double take. "What happened to you two?"

From the couch, Nate and Dante's heads popped around. "Jun, is that blood?"

"Someone threw an egg at Holly," he responded, not answering the question.

Minhyuk abandoned the bag of sugar, wiping his hands on his apron as he hurried over. "Are you OK?" he asked, peering at the back of my head.

I nodded, wincing. "I headbutted Jun. That hurts more."

"Do we need to go to a hospital?" Dante asked.

I shot him a look of disbelief. "Unless the egg had a knife inside it and it's embedded in the back of my head, no, a hospital is not needed. And Jun's nose has already stopped bleeding."

Dante waved his hand dismissively. "The maknae will bounce back. I'm more worried about you."

"Still don't need a hospital," I said, dryly. "I need to wash my hair, and maybe take a couple of painkillers."

"Jun, grab a chair," Minhyuk instructed the younger member.

I held my hands up. "OK, Jun, you need to sit down for a bit and make sure that the nosebleed doesn't start up."

"I will look after Jun," Dante assured me. "You must let Minhyuk look after you."

"I literally need a shower," I sighed.

"I will help," Minhyuk assured me, nodding at Nate.

My eyes went wide. "Shower?"

Nate, chair in hand, led the way to the bathroom, and set the chair down so it was facing away from the sink. Minhyuk, who had been guiding me down the hallway, ignoring my protests, sat me down in it. Gently he pushed my head back, scooping up my hair. "Just relax," he muttered.

"I can take a shower, you know," I pointed out. "I didn't lose any arms or legs during this." I folded my arms and stared grouchily up at the ceiling.

"You want a shower," Minhyuk said as he started the water running.

"I just said that," I pointed out, dryly.

"Only you will naturally have the water hot."

I nodded. "It's not really an occasion that calls for a cold shower."

"And then you will have scrambled egg in your hair, which will be much harder to get out."

I opened my mouth, then fell silent. OK, he had a point. He leaned over and peered down at me. "Fine," I conceded when he gave me a pointed look.

"Just relax," he grinned, before pouring tepid water over me.

I shivered. There was no way I would have been able to endure a shower like this. While Minhyuk worked away at my hair, Nate gently draped a towel over me, then stood by, dabbing at any water that ran astray before it went down my face or neck. I closed my eyes. If the water was a tiny bit warmer, Minhyuk's fingers in my hair would have been an amazing feeling.

As if he knew what I was thinking, the water went warmer and the scent of my shampoo filled my nose. Before I could stop myself, a moan escaped me.

"What the hell is going on here?" My head shot up, sending soapy water everywhere, as I found Tae in the doorway.

"Someone attacked Holly," Minhyuk answered for me.

"They threw an egg at me," I clarified, as Jun, Dante, and Kyun appeared behind him. Suddenly, the bathroom was feeling very crowded.

"Why?" Tae asked.

"I think that was my fault," Jun muttered.

Tae turned on the spot to glower at Jun. "Why?" he demanded.

Ignoring the water that was streaming down me, I stood, holding my hands up. "OK, let's not jump to conclusions. I don't think it was your fault, Jun."

"You were talking to me," he shrugged.

"Yes, but the normal reaction for anyone when they witness two people talking to each other is not usually to throw an egg at one of them."

"Who threw an egg at you?" Tae asked, rounding back to me.

I shook my head. "I don't know," I said, honestly. "I think she was a fan. She knew who Jun was. I think she got a little excited at seeing her idol, and then a little jealous at seeing him with me," I continued, calmly. "As soon as Jun pointed out I was his manager, she ran away."

"What were you doing for her to be jealous at seeing you together?" Nate asked from behind. I turned to him and found him staring at me with his head cocked.

"We were discussing going out for food this evening, seeing as we didn't go last night," I said, conveniently leaving out the fact I had been waiting on Jun kissing me. Aside from the fact that I didn't want to upset Nate ... or Tae ... lord, this was a mess ... aside from that, Jun was already feeling guilty when he didn't need to be. "Anyway, I'm choosing to see this as a good thing."

Tae stared at me like I was crazy. "How hard did that egg hit you?"

From beside me, both Nate and Minhyuk were trying to get me to sit back down. I did as they insisted but sighed in the process. "Don't get me wrong, this hurt, and could have been a lot worse if it had hit Jun."

Dante snorted. "Doubt it. His head's soft enough."

"Hey!" Jun objected.

"You have fans!" I pointed out. "OK, you have some slightly crazy fans, and I will be discussing that part at Atlantis later, but for now, just be happy that people know who you are. This means you're getting popular. So, instead of you all watching me wash my hair, why don't you go and take advantage of this. Go write some songs." I frowned. "Actually, go check the views on the music video. We should do something to thank your fans. Go think of a way to do a special dance practice video. They'd love that."

That finally got them to leave the room, so it was just Minhyuk, who had resumed washing my hair, and Nate, who was doing his best to dab as much of the soapy water dry. I closed my eyes and chewed at my lip. I'd said all that because I hadn't wanted the guys to worry. The last thing I wanted was for them to feel unsafe as they walked the streets, but the truth was, *I* was worried. I was grateful their popularity had swung upwards, but if the cost was some crazy girls doing stupid stuff like that, I needed to make sure they were safe.

H3RO

I had a meeting with the Atlantis security team first thing the following morning. They assured me they would look into it. Feeling better, I returned to the dorms to pick Dante up.

I'd gotten a call from a designer brand asking for Dante to be a model for their underwear. I had checked there were no restrictions in his contract, which there weren't. When I'd floated the idea past the group's

Chinese member, he had grinned like I had told him he had won the lottery, and accepted straight away.

He was still wearing a smug grin when he slipped into the minibus. The shoot was in one of the most exclusive hotels in the city, which thankfully came with underground valet parking.

We walked into the hotel, and I did my best to hide my amazement. No expense had been spared here. A rep from the company greeted us and led us over to the elevator, explaining how they had a suite on the 42nd floor at their disposal. I was more interested in the sign for the Michelin-starred Chinese restaurant on the top floor. I had missed breakfast and I was already hungry.

It was a quick ride to the suite, and inside, my mouth fell open. It was beautiful. Tastefully decorated with lots of cream and sleek lines. "Mister Feng, this way please," an assistant said, ushering us to one of the bedrooms. Inside, it had been set up with several areas for hair and makeup.

Leaving Dante to it, I took a seat at the dining table, out of the way of the shoot. I got my head down getting some work done … and then Dante walked out in nothing but a pair of black boxer briefs …

Holy hell, I was not getting any work done this afternoon.

I must have been completely absorbed in my work, as I hadn't realized how much time had passed since we had sat down. They had dyed Dante's hair back to black, covering up the fading red streaks that had been there for the 'Who Is Your Hero?' video. They'd straightened it and trimmed it, so it was longer in the back but wasn't quite the mullet style that seemed to be popular at the moment. Half of his fringe had been pushed to the side, showing off his beautiful eyes, now sporting blue contacts.

Dante had a set of abs on him which honestly had me appreciating the term 'washboard abs'. The lines of his torso were exceptionally defined. His body was the typical triangle shape, however it wasn't as broad as Nate's. Curling around his neck was the end of the dragon's tail tattoo. I was surprised, but happy that they hadn't hidden it with makeup. Unfortunately, tattoos were still taboo in Korea so I had a feeling it was going to get photoshopped out.

My eyes traced lower, drinking in his pale skin, pausing at the briefs.

I was well aware of what hung under there. And holy hell, did it hang. I licked my lips, before I could stop myself, then I pulled myself from the X-rated images which were beginning to form in my head. Images which had my tongue being put to other uses. I shook my head. I was his manager. I had enough … who the hell knew what to call it … stuff … going on with Jun and Nate.

Tae had been taken off that list. With his reaction to who my family was, and his lack of trust, that bridge was burned. Given how I had a list to start with, I should have been relieved at that. Now that he was upset with me—that certainly didn't fill me with any relief— I didn't need to worry about hurting him further with what was happening (what *was* happening?) between myself, Jun and Nate.

I glanced up and caught Dante's eyes. There was no way on this earth he had any idea that my mind was full of images of me and him, but with the satisfied smirk he was giving me, I was half sure he had developed psychic abilities. Either that or I had been extremely obvious in my appreciation.

I cleared my throat, and then diverted my attention to the iPad I had been working from. *Stop staring!* I instructed myself.

I listened to that voice for all of five minutes—until the photographer started ordering Dante around. *Holy hell*, that man was gorgeous. He was one of those guys who just screamed sex. No matter what pose he struck, and the photographer, Pablo, had him posing all around the room, Dante delivered. I had a feeling that when I saw the final images—or even the proofs, every single one of those pictures would have him silently asking the viewer if he could fuck them.

I wasn't quite sure how that would sell underwear, but then I figured it might encourage the woman to buy the underwear for their boyfriends or husbands. Sex sold bras, right? Look at Victoria's Secret.

I questioned it for all of ten seconds, and then returned my attention to Dante. Who the hell cared?

And that was just the first set of underwear.

By the end of the shoot, several hours later, the dress I was wearing felt far too tight fitting and it had quite a floaty skirt to it. While Dante disappeared back into the bedroom to get dressed, the photographer's assistant came over to thank me for waiting patiently, like he knew how torturous it had been … well, he probably did.

"The hotel has several private rooms in the restaurant. We had some booked out for Pablo, but we're flying out to Tokyo tonight instead. One is yours if you want it?" he offered. "And it's all already paid for."

"That sounds great," I agreed with a smile. There was no way I was turning down free food, especially not from a Michelin-starred Chinese restaurant. I slipped my iPad into my purse, then hurried over to the bedroom to share the good news with Dante.

The room was empty, aside from the temporary hair and makeup stations which were still set up. I frowned, glancing around. Was there another door into the room? The only other one I could see was the bathroom. "Dante?" I called.

Dante stuck his head around the bathroom door. He quickly scanned the room and stepped out.

Naked.

"Do you even own clothes?" I spluttered.

"This is so much more freeing," he shrugged, leaning against the door frame. "And if you've got it, flaunt it."

He definitely had it. I couldn't stop myself from staring. He pulled himself away from the door frame and sauntered over. I swallowed, doing my best to keep my eyes firmly on his as he leaned forward. "I know," he whispered in my ear.

My mouth fell open. "Did I say that out loud?"

Dante stepped back, smirking. "You didn't need to. I see the way you stare at me."

"I do not stare!" I lied, spinning around so my back was to him. Mentally, I kicked myself. We both knew that I had spent the entire afternoon staring.

제4 장

H3Rㅇ

Seoul Night

By the time we walked out of the suite, I knew the last thing I needed to do was be alone with Dante. The short ride in the elevator to the top floor felt like it took an eternity, rather than seconds. There was an energy—an electricity—to the air, which left me feeling hot and bothered. Dante was leaning lazily against the wall, staring at me, doing nothing to hide the fact he was obviously thinking filthy thoughts.

I, on the other hand, was doing a much better job at hiding that. In that, I was trying. I wasn't sure I was succeeding …

The hostess led us through the restaurant to a short hallway, and a room off it. It was a small room with a low wall halfway down. We were led to the other side, and I couldn't keep myself from gasping at the sight. The wall was the back to the booth, looking out at a window which had the most incredible view of Seoul in the twilight.

I slid behind the table, trying to keep the long silky-feeling tablecloth from catching underneath me as I shuffled around. Dante slid in next to me, keeping close.

"Your server will be in shortly," the hostess announced before leaving us.

I was already pulling out my phone, taking pictures of the view. "This place is beautiful." I turned, slowly, taking pictures of the room. I stopped when I found Dante staring at me. I cocked an eyebrow at him. "Please tell me this isn't the part where you tell me I'm more beautiful," I asked, dryly.

Dante looked down at himself, and then back at me. "You know I'm not Jun, right?"

I laughed. "Fair." That did sound more like something that Jun would come out with.

He leaned forward. "Besides, you still need to admit you like what you see."

"Have you seen that view?" I asked, purposely ignoring his point. "That's incredible."

"Oh, I see how you want to play it," he smirked. He leaned forward, bringing his mouth to my ear. I couldn't stop the shiver that ran down me. "I'll be right back," he whispered, before gently biting my lobe.

Before I could question him, he had slipped under the table, disappearing behind the table cloth. "Dante!" I hissed, as the door behind me opened. All of a sudden, a hand wrapped around each leg, just behind my knee, pulling me to the edge of the seat. I had to stop myself from squealing in fright as the waitress stepped around the table.

"Good evening," she greeted me. She had been pulling a small cart which was covered in table items.

"Hi," I responded, hoping to hell she had no idea where Dante was. Then Dante's hands started traveling up my legs, under the skirt. My hands shot down to grab his, just as they toyed with the edge of my underwear. At the same time, I brought my torso flush with the edge of the table.

"Ma'am?"

"I'm sorry, I haven't had chance to look at the menu," I told her. She blinked at me a few times, and it took me a moment to realize I'd spoken to her in English.

Before I could change language, she nodded. "There is no menu," she replied, also in English.

At that, one of Dante's hand slipped out of my grasp, then moved so he was holding both my hands in place using one of his. Meanwhile, his other hand brushed over the fabric of my panties. "What?" I squeaked.

The waitress nodded, politely. How the hell did she not have a clue what was happening? "You will be served six courses over the next hour. There is no need to worry about making those decisions."

Below the table, under my skirt, Dante's fingers played with the edge of the elastic, and then they were slowly being tugged down. "What are you doing?" I demanded, before I could stop myself.

The waitress looked at me in alarm. "Setting up for the first course," she said, apologetically. "I'm sorry this was not ready when you were seated."

I went to clamp my legs together, but somehow, Dante stopped me. "I'm sorry, I didn't mean to shout at you," I apologized, quickly. There was a sharp yank, and then my underwear was halfway down my thigh. I was going to murder him. "I was just expecting a little more warning," I said, though my words were aimed at Dante as I kicked lightly at him.

"I will be right back with your first course," the waitress said, wheeling the now empty cart away, just as my underwear was pulled to my ankles.

As soon as the door closed behind her, I ducked my head under the table. "What in the holy hell are you doing?" I demanded.

Dante grinned up at me. "Don't pretend you're not turned on right now, because these are soaking," he declared, holding my panties up with a finger.

"That's not—"

"Holly, just to be clear, the only thing I want to eat right now, is you. So, shut up, quit pretending like you haven't imaged my head between your legs all afternoon, and enjoy."

"Dante," I started, trying to get my brain to work as he shifted under the table, settling the backs of my knees on his shoulders. "What if the waitress comes back?"

Dante smirked up at me. "*When* she comes back in, you might want to try biting your lip." He shrugged, his hands moving me closer to the edge of the booth's seat, pushing my legs further apart. "Or don't."

His mouth moved towards me, and I only just had the sense to grip at the edge of the table as his tongue licked at the tops of my thighs. His fingers ran up and down the outside of my legs, then slowly moved upwards.

"Oh, hell," I murmured, staring out across Seoul. He was right. I *was* turned on. I *did* want this, and although I hadn't quite imagined it like *this*. I *had* imagined it. What was worse, was that I was already close to an orgasm.

The door opened, and as it did, Dante ran a single

thumb between my slit, skimming so lightly over the already sensitive area, I clutched tighter at the table, trying hard not to make a sound. I could feel Dante's silent laughter against the skin of my thighs.

"Your partner is still not here?" the waitress asked.

I shook my head. "He had to step out," I told her.

"Shall I serve the first course?" she asked in concern, glancing down at the cart she had pushed in.

"That's fine," I told her. She nodded, turning to reach for the bowls. Beneath the table, Dante gently spread my lips, and ran his tongue all the way along me. "Oh!" I gasped, just as the waitress turned back to me. She set one of the bowls in front of me, giving me a look of confusion. "That looks good," I quickly said, trying my hardest to appear natural. She gave me a small smile, and I picked up the spoon. As she turned back for the other bowl, Dante's tongue sucked at my clit. I bit down on my lip, hard, as a burst of pleasure shot through me.

"Is everything OK, ma'am?" she asked, setting the second bowl down.

I nodded, not trusting myself to speak as Dante continued to tease me. I had always assumed I was the kind of girl would never do anything like this, but here I was, fighting my body to stop from having an orgasm in front of her. The risk of her finding out, and the almost public display of it all, was making this the most exhilarating and erotic thing I had ever experienced.

"Your first course is a twice-boiled chicken broth soup with male sturgeon maw and scallops," she informed me.

"Uh-huh," I managed. At this point, she could

have been serving me burned mac and cheese, and I wouldn't have cared. I didn't need a description to go with it. I need her to get lost, pronto, so I could orgasm.

"I am serving it with a chilled Corton-Charlemagne …"

I stopped listening, staring at her nodding my head as my lower lip went numb from where I was biting down. A hand shot under the table, trying to push Dante's head away for a reprieve. Thankfully, he pulled back, switching his attention to sucking on one of my fingers. The breath of relief almost exploded from me. "Thank you," I said, cutting off whatever she had been saying about pairing the wine with the soup.

She gave me a small smile, then stepped back. "Enjoy." Before she had gotten around the back of the booth, Dante's tongue was back to teasing me. The door closed with a soft click, and just like that, he pulled back.

"Dante!" I exclaimed, all hot and bothered and desperately wanting to feel that release.

"Admit it," he requested from under the table.

"What?" I demanded, the frustration getting to me.

"That you like what you see."

I jerked the tablecloth up, glowering at him between my legs. "Are you serious right now?" He had the audacity to wiggle an eyebrow at me. "Yes," I growled. "I like what I see. I did the moment I laid my eyes on every glorious inch of you, now stop being a god damn tease!"

Laughing to himself, he returned his mouth to where I desperately needed it. When he slipped a couple of fingers inside me, moving them in time with his tongue, I snatched at my napkin, bringing it up to muffle my cries as I couldn't fight back my orgasm any longer.

Below the table, Dante continued to lick, lapping up the waves of my orgasm. I collapsed back against the booth, convinced my bones had disappeared from my body, as I stared out over the now night skyline.

The tremors slowly subsided as Dante finally extracted himself from under the table. He sat down beside me, pulling the napkin from me, and using it to delicately dab at the side of his mouth.

"I hate you," I muttered, unable to manage more than that.

"No, you really don't," he grinned at me.

"Arrogance isn't attractive," I grumbled.

He leaned over, helping me back into an upright position, before kissing me. I could taste the hint of me in his mouth and *holy hell*, my body was responding to him again.

Just like that, he pulled away and picked up a spoon, taking a mouthful of soup. I let out a whimper of complaint—an actual whimper. Dante smirked at me but only continued eating his soup.

I reached for my own spoon and tried a bit. It wasn't the nicest of chicken soups I'd had, but all of a sudden, I was ravenous. I devoured the small bowl in no time.

Overall, the meal was good. It was full of flavors and well prepared, but none of it left me as satisfied as Dante had. Every so often, he would lean over and mutter something in my ear. He always spoke in Mandarin and I had no idea what he said, but I was certain, judging from the expression on his face, it was dirty.

"Are you going to translate any of that?" I asked, as we finished our final course.

"No," he said, leaning in towards me. "But one day I may show you."

"Oh, you'd better," I whispered as he nibbled at my ear.

"I will," he promised. He pulled away, then slid out from behind the table, offering me a hand to help me out.

It wasn't until I was standing that I realized something important. "My underwear!" I hissed at him.

He shook his head. "They're mine now." He patted at a pocket. I made to snatch at them, but the waitress walked back in.

"Thank you for visiting us. I hope you enjoyed your meal and will come again."

Dante gestured with his hand that I should lead. Shooting him a glare first, I did so. Behind me, I heard him say to the waitress. "She will."

I waited until we were in the elevator before I punched his arm. "She will?" I repeated. "It's a good job she had no idea what was going on."

"Please," he scoffed. "She knew exactly what was going on, and you know it."

I refused to look at him. Partly because I was embarrassed, partly because he was right, but mostly because I was getting turned on again.

The door pinged open and Dante took my hand, leading me through the reception lobby to the valet parking. While we were waiting, Dante turned to me. "We should do that again."

A cool breeze whipped around my legs and up my

skirt. I quickly crossed my legs, making sure to hold the skirt down. "Was there really a need to steal my underwear?" I hissed at him as the car was brought around.

제5장

H3RՕ

Take A Shot

"You've been gone ages," Minhyuk announced as we walked into the dorm. "I didn't know what to cook you, so I was going to make ramyun for you."

"I've already eaten," Dante declared, giving me a pointed look. "I'd go for seconds of that though?"

"Maybe next time," I told him, forcing myself not to react as Dante slowly licked his lips. I couldn't help but start to replay our earlier encounter. Who was I trying to fool? I was down for seconds too.

"What did you eat?" Minhyuk asked. His question was completely innocent, but his curiosity had me focusing my attention anywhere but at Dante as I quickly remembered we weren't the only ones in the room. My gaze dropped on Jun.

Once again, he was staring intently between Dante and me. "I have a feeling I'd like it," Jun said, his gaze fixing onto me.

My lips parted slowly at the heat in his stare, and the lack of underwear was doing nothing to stop me getting turned on. Before I could find an appropriate response, Dante grinned. "I can assure you it is one of the sweetest things you'll ever taste."

"Where did you go?" Minhyuk asked again.

"The Chinese restaurant at the top of the Tower Hotel," I quickly told him. "We had their six-course meal after the shoot was finished."

"It was sweet?" Minhyuk asked in surprise.

"I had a seventh course," Dante shrugged.

Minhyuk turned to me, cocking his head. "Couldn't you manage a seventh course? What was it?"

"Too much for Holly to handle." I nearly choked on the air I was breathing.

I whirled around and jabbed his ribs. "Really?"

Dante just chuckled before sauntering down the hallway to the bedroom he shared with Minhyuk. I closed my eyes and sucked in a deep breath. I wasn't sure if I wanted to follow him for a second round, or to kill him. "It has been a long day," I mumbled, thankful that Minhyuk, at least, seemed to have no clue about any of the innuendo.

I hurried to my own room, closing the door and leaning against it. My heart was pounding, and I was starting to feel hot and bothered again. I had work I needed to do, especially as I had spent most of the afternoon staring at Dante instead of my iPad, but I was honestly considering giving myself some intimate relief first. I wasn't sure I was capable of focusing on my emails right now.

Behind me, there was a knock at the door. I dropped my head to my chest. The universe had other plans.

I turned and opened the door, surprised to find Jun there. "Is everything OK?" I asked him, slowly. He glanced down the corridor, then stepped into my room, his movements making me take a couple of hurried steps out of the way. "Jun?"

He closed the door behind him, then turned suddenly. "I just need to remind you of something."

"What's …?" the question died in my throat as Jun advanced towards me. Oh, there was no way in hell I had forgotten anything when it came to Jun, despite the fact my brain was constantly reminding me that what I was doing wasn't fair, especially considering all I had done with the others in the group. The same group.

Despite the fact I emitted a vocal complaint at my own actions, I stepped back. "Jun, there's something you need to know," I tried to tell him.

Jun paused. "Are the next words you say going to be that you do not want me to kiss you?" I swallowed, then shook my head. "Then I don't care," he shrugged. I had genuinely been about to tell him that he wasn't the only one I was doing things with, but he pulled me to him and captured my mouth with his.

His kiss was fierce, his teeth tugging and teasing at my lips, yet, even when I parted them, he didn't use his tongue. I moaned in frustration, my hands seeking out handfuls of his shirt, pulling him closer. Just as he finally dipped his tongue in my mouth, there was a knock at the door.

I leaped back, my face feeling hot and flustered as I dabbed at it with the back of my hand. "Damnit," I cursed under my breath. "Just a moment," I called out as Jun smirked to himself.

"Holly, we have a problem," Tae called through the door, the handle starting to move.

"I'm just getting changed!" I cried as the door

started to open. It shut in a second.

"Sorry," Tae apologized. "Please come out when you're ready. It's urgent."

Alarmed at the worried tone Tae was using, I hurried over, pulling it open a crack. Tae wasn't there. Confident I wasn't going to have to explain why Jun was in my room if I left now, I ducked out and jogged down the hallway to the living room.

Tae, Dante, Nate, Minhyuk, and Kyun were all standing around the kitchen island as I entered the room, staring down at something. "What's wrong?"

Silently, Dante picked up the iPad the group used for their SNS and handed it over. It was open to a Korean tabloid site. My eyes fell on a picture of me and Dante outside of the hotel, holding hands. That had to have been just over an hour ago.

H3RO's Dante caught leaving hotel with mysterious woman.

I stared at the picture with the sensation of my heart plummeting into my stomach.

"Clearly, we know it's not an issue," Tae said, acting like that was the most natural response to Dante and I caught together. "You are our manager, after all."

"What is the issue?" Jun asked, joining my side. He took the iPad from me and scanned the article before his gaze settled on me.

"We don't need a scandal midway through our promotions," Kyun snapped at him, irritably. "We don't need a scandal at all."

Jun shrugged. "I don't see an issue with her being with any of us."

I turned my attention from Kyun to Jun at his words. There was something about how he had said that which felt … odd. Before I could work out what it was, Kyun was walking over, jabbing at the screen. "Of course not. She's our manager. It's natural that she's seen with us."

That was what was off with Jun's sentence: it was missing the word seen.

"That's the problem," Kyun continued. "She's our manager. How do people not know this? More importantly, why has Atlantis not said anything?"

I sighed and moved over to the fridge to seek out a bottle of water. "Does it really matter if people know who I am?" I asked them. I turned back, unscrewing the cap. "As you said, I'm your manager, not a member of H3RO. I'd rather you guys were getting the attention."

"Holly, they reached out to Atlantis for a statement and they refused to comment," Minhyuk pointed out. I hadn't read that much of the article.

Tae nodded. "It wouldn't take much for them to set this straight, yet instead, they're leaving this open and causing us more problems. Have you read the comments?"

I'd barely read the article. I hadn't even scrolled through the comments section. I shook my head. "It's late. Maybe there's no one there."

"You're Lee Woojin's daughter," Kyun said in disbelief. "You're the daughter of the Chairman of Atlantis Entertainment," he added as though his first statement needed further clarification. "They might not care about us being caught up in a scandal, but they would surely do something for you."

I sank back against the fridge and shrugged. "There's no need to sound so outraged," I told him with another shrug. "I'm the illegitimate child, don't forget.

To say Sejin hates me is quite honestly an understatement. He won't give two thoughts about how I look in all of this, just like he won't care about you guys." I sighed and set the bottle down on the counter to the side of me. "I'll reach out to the site and let them know who I am though. You're right—none of you need to be caught up in a scandal. I'm sorry."

"Why are you apologizing?" Dante demanded. "I'm the one there with you and I don't care what people think."

"You should," Kyun snapped at him. "The last thing we want is to upset our fans."

I nodded. "I'll get a statement issued, and explain who I am." Actually, I was going to do more than that. I pulled out my phone and hunted down the article. It wasn't hard—it was the top trending. Rolling my eyes, I copied the link and sent it to Lee Woojin. The response was instant: **Consider it handled.** "Done," I told them.

"Holly," Dante started, but I shook my head at him.

"Don't worry about it too much, guys," I said, giving them a reassuring smile. "Now, if you'll excuse me, I am exhausted and I really need to get some sleep. Seeing as you have a show tomorrow, I suggest you all do the same too." Swiping up my bottle of water, I returned to my room.

I had barely pulled on a pair of pajamas when there was a soft rap at the door. I walked over, prepared to tell Jun I just wanted sleep now, but found someone else at the door. "Tae?" I said, peering up at him in confusion.

"Your brother doesn't like you."

He was watching me with his intense, sad eyes.

For the first time since he had found out who my family was, they weren't filled with betrayal. "I'm fairly certain he's actively trying to find a way to get rid of me," I shrugged, wearily. "So, saying he doesn't like me is probably an understatement."

"Does H3RO's success mean it will ruin your relationship with him?"

I chuckled, dryly. "Tae, we don't have a relationship to ruin. There was a point, very early on, that I was curious about my family and if things had started out on better footing, then maybe I'd be upset about that."

He stared down at me, considering my words. "There are already hideous comments about you on SNS and he did nothing to protect you."

Hideous? Just how bad were they? "Right now, I'm a nobody, Tae," I shrugged. "If he tells the world who I am, the world then knows that the heir to the Atlantis Entertainment fortune has an illegitimate competitor. He's not going to want to announce that."

"But by getting your father to do it, you will be opening yourself up to that attention," he pointed out.

I sucked in a breath. I hadn't thought about that. My life was already more complicated than some of the dramas I'd watched, but when that news broke … I shrugged. "I would rather they focus on that than negatively on H3RO." I reached over and rested my hand on his arm. "Look, if it gets bad, I will find you guys another manager. I know you don't trust me anymore, but I hope you can believe me when I say I won't let my family drama damage H3RO. I hope I can help you get that second number one I promised first, but if my name is going to hinder that, I will back out to give you all a fighting chance."

"I don't ... I don't not trust you," Tae said, quietly. "Holly, I'm still hurt you lied. But I do think you have H3RO's best interests at heart. H3RO can handle the gossip. We'll protect you."

And then he disappeared, leaving me staring in disbelief at the door he had closed behind him.

My life was a giant rollercoaster of emotional ups and downs.

I got into bed and pulled out my iPad, seeking out the article so I could read the comments. The ones on the English-speaking sites had relatively positive comments ranging from *where have H3RO been all my life* to *Dante is pure sex on legs* (they weren't wrong) and *I have just found my new Ult* to the equally positive of *I'm gutted, but I'm happy Dante is happy* or *It was supposed to be me—she'd best treat him right.*

I was taking the latter as positive, although I was questioning just how well I was treating him when there was Nate and Jun in the picture.

And then I moved to the Korean-speaking sites...

These comments were brutal. There were very few positive comments, with the few that were there echoing the sentiments of the English-speaking ones. The rest, however, were attacking me—specifically my appearance. There were a lot of comments saying I was far too ugly to even be breathing the same air. Many more were saying Dante was too good for me and he could do better (one politely pointing out that a trash can would be a better alternative and less likely to be carrying germs).

Then there were the ones that called Dante a traitor for cheating on his fans. There were even a few comments directed at him being Chinese, and how it was only natural for him to have lower standards—but he shouldn't be reflecting badly on H3RO. Those upset me the most.

The article had been updated a very short time ago, but the timestamp of the comments was from when it had been first published. No wonder they had been worried.

I quickly read the updated article. It now included a short press release to state I was H3RO's manager, and although I was from America where **"behavior such as hand-holding is considered normal between the opposite sex, [I] was deeply apologetic for [my] actions as [I] had not considered the effect this behavior would have on H3RO's fans."** There was more to say I would reflect and I would ensure that there would be no more behavior such as this.

Honestly, I wasn't sure if I was upset or grateful at that. Realizing that I did have different standards as to what was normal behavior between two people of the opposite sex, and that really, it was easy to see how they were upset, I leaned towards grateful.

Even more obvious was the fact that I was his manager. Regardless of what was normal behavior between friends or … whatever the hell we were … the simple fact was I was his *manager*.

I was going to go check on Dante and make sure he was alright, but I spotted the time and stopped myself. I had been lost in comments for hours. I would check on him in the morning and hoped he wasn't too upset by what was being said.

I took another look at the statement and realized something else. At no point was it mentioned who I was. My father had managed to deliver that statement without admitting I was his child.

I wasn't sure how I felt about that on a personal level, but at least it was one less thing to draw negative attention to H3RO. That, I was thankful for.

제6 장

H3RO

Road To Stardom

Today's show was *Seoul Nights*. Despite the article from the night before, everyone seemed to be in good spirits: the show was one where they would perform and interact with the hosts and the audience, so H3RO were looking forward to it.

I had managed to speak to Dante who said he refused to read any comments on social media, and therefore wasn't concerned. I wasn't sure if I believed him. If I'd found out people were leaving comments about me (which I had), then I would check them (which I did). His third language may have been Korean, but he would know what was said if he did read them. However, he seemed to be happy to let it be forgotten about, so I didn't want to push it.

I had taken screen shots of them all though and filed them away. Hopefully this would be the end of it, but I knew that regardless of whether an article was positive or negative, there would be people who simply didn't like H3RO and would leave hateful messages anyway. If I caught a whiff of a repeat offender, I was going to find out who they were and press charges.

I parked the minibus in an assigned space and took the lead for the group. The path to the studio was lined with fans, safely behind metal barriers, but the route was designed for fans to see their idols. We were ahead of schedule, so I wasn't worried when H3RO started wandering over to chat with them.

It was sweet. They tried to say hello to as many of them as possible. They weren't as big as BTS or Wanna One, but there was a big enough crowd that even at the thinnest areas, the barriers were still lined.

H3RO made their way along the line, being patient with the shyer fans, and making sure to say hello to their fanboys. Jun gave the biggest grin when one of them declared his love in a loud shout. He turned to Minhyuk, teasing him that he was loved more, and in response, another fanboy shouted his love for Minhyuk. I laughed, unable to stop myself as the pair teased each other.

They didn't have many opportunities like this to interact with their fans, as most of the time, the schedules didn't allow for it. I ended up giving them too much time and a show executive appeared in the doorway, waving us in with a scowl on his face.

"Guys, I'm sorry, but you need to go in now," I called over to them. That earned me a chorus of boos and jeers. I turned to the fans and bowed my head apologetically. "I am sorry, but they must keep to their schedule."

I got H3RO inside the building and to hair and makeup. Then I allowed myself to relax while they filmed. As they were busy, I wandered back to the green room, seeking out a bottle of water from their rider. I was standing at the window, drinking, when I noticed the crowd outside.

In the few hours we had been inside, it had doubled.

That had never happened before.

It left me feeling uneasy. There were only a handful of security, and they were associated with the studio. Chewing at my lip, I pulled out my phone and dialed the Atlantis switchboard, asking to be put through to the security manager.

He was the one I had spoken to when the egg had been thrown at me. I didn't like him. He didn't seem the slightest bit concerned when I told him the crowd had grown, and then informed me that they wouldn't be able to get anyone out to us at this late stage.

Outside, the crowd was continuing to grow. As was the knot of worry in my stomach.

By the time H3RO had finished, I was pacing back and forth in front of the window. The crowd was massive. Yes, it was amazing that H3RO was this popular, but those metal barriers were not secure. While H3RO were gathering their things together so we could leave, I sought out one of the show executives.

"Do you have another exit?" I asked him.

"Why?" he asked, curiously.

I led him over to a window and used my chin to nod down at the still growing crowd below. "Unless you have extra security? I put in a request from Atlantis, but they cannot get here in time."

"We don't have the resources for that," the exec said, his eyes growing wide. He looked back to me and nodded. "If you can bring the minibus around, we can have you leave via the loading bay on the opposite side of the building."

"Thank you," I said in relief. "That would be …" I trailed off as an amazing sound made its way up to our floor.

"Is that what I think it is?" Minhyuk asked, bounding over to my side. He pulled open one of the windows and the sound of the crowd singing their song, 'Who Is Your Hero?' became clearer.

My mouth fell open as the other members of H3RO joined myself and Minhyuk. It was … beautiful.

"Now might be a good time to move your minibus," the exec murmured in my ear.

Before I started crying, I decided that was a good idea. "Please could you bring H3RO down?" I asked after being given careful instruction on how to get the minibus to the loading bay. After he agreed, I tapped Tae on the shoulder. He turned to me, grinning. "I don't want to take you guys out through that," I informed him. "We don't have enough security."

"OK," Tae agreed, simply. "But it's a wonderful sight."

"And sound," I agreed, listening to the singing as it continued. "They're loud."

I left them to listen and hurried downstairs, using a side door to exit and collect the minibus. The crowds were thick with people and I had to weave my way through with force, although they were standing calmly singing at the tops of their lungs, none would move out the way, as though they would lose their place.

I was two thirds of the way to the van when the crowd stopped singing, instead screaming in excitement. "It's Dante!" someone screeched in my ear.

In a panic, I turned to the door, terrified at the thought that Dante had followed me. There was no one behind me. I glanced up, then relaxed a fraction when I saw him at the window, using the team's iPad to record the crowd below.

He gave me a wave, and the crowd erupted into excited screams again. "He waved at me!" one girl yelled at her friend.

I winced at the noise and kept my head down, moving as fast as I could through the excited crowds, finally breaking free on the other side where the minibus was parked. I started the engine and glanced back at the crowd. Thankfully, everyone was still focusing their attention on the window where Minhyuk had now joined Dante.

I drove the minibus around and waited. A few minutes later, the six members of H3RO were safely in the minibus with me. I let out a sigh of relief. "You guys are pretty popular," I told Minhyuk. He was in the front seat with me.

"Did you hear them singing our song?" he asked, his eyes alight with excitement.

As I waited for a barrier to go up, I turned to him and arched an eyebrow. "I'm sorry, I can't hear you. I was deafened by screams," I told him, dryly.

"Uh, guys," Nate leaned forward between the seats. I glanced down and found him pointing. I followed his finger, just in time to witness maybe twenty fans come running down the exit ramp.

My hand shot to the door lock, slamming it down. I turned to Minhyuk, who looked as alarmed as I felt. "Do me a favor and move into the back?"

He nodded, and with some help from Nate, squeezed himself through as the crowd swarmed around the van. Before I would work out what to do, they were hammering at the windows, trying to open the doors: I was glad I'd hit the lock when I had!

I beeped at the horn, hoping that would scare them off.

It didn't.

I tried again, this time trying to inch the van forward. The fans didn't move, so I stopped: I really didn't want to hurt anyone.

I swallowed, trying to keep calm.

I hadn't been prepared for this.

I glanced in the rearview mirror, unintentionally catching Nate's eye. He leaned forward, discreetly placing his hand on my shoulder. I closed my eyes, sucking in a deep breath. Then I pulled my phone out of my pocket and called the police, somehow remaining calm as I explained the situation.

I turned back to the others. They all looked scared, although some were doing a better job of hiding it than others. "I'm sorry," I told them. "We'll be able to leave soon."

"It's not your fault," Minhyuk told me, ducking his head as a flash went off at the window.

It felt like it was my fault though. I had seen the crowd and I'd expected something to happen. I should have done more to stop this: it was literally my job. I glanced into the mirrors, trying to see around me. We were completely surrounded.

I sucked in another deep breath, trying to calm myself and work out what I could do. I toyed with the idea of stepping out of the minibus, or even cracking the window open to ask them to move back, but then decided against it. There weren't *that* many of them, but I had a feeling these were the hardcore fans which would do anything to just touch their idols.

Finally, the police turned up: two cars with three officers in each. As soon as they pulled up, lights flashing, half of the fans bolted. Of those that remained, most moved away from the minibus when the police walked over. It was only a couple who had to be led away.

An officer tapped on my window, making me jump. I wound it down so he could speak to me. "Are you OK?" he asked me.

I nodded, glancing back at the others. They all nodded their agreements. "Yes," I told him. "Thank you."

"We cannot arrest any of them unless the studio would like to press charges for trespassing," he said, almost apologetically.

"Can you get names?" I requested. "Just so I know if there are future instances."

The officer gave me a wary look, but nodded. "You should have better security if you think there will be future instances," he informed me.

"I intend on seeing to that," I assured him, handing over a business card with all my contact information on it.

While I did this, a door opened behind. I whirled around in panic, just as Minhyuk returned to his seat in the front. "There wasn't a spare seat back there," he explained before I could yell at him.

"Smart man," the officer nodded. He turned back to me. "I will need to take your statement."

"I want to get H3RO back to the dorms," I told him. "I will come to the precinct after, if that's OK?"

The officer nodded. "You should also check your

vehicle for damage." He glanced up and down the minibus with a frown. "It looks pretty beaten up."

I gave him an awkward smile. The minibus was a lump of junk. The damage had probably been inflicted long before we had left for the morning.

I wanted to get out of there while the police were still there to keep an eye on things. I waited to be waved off, and then left. We drove in silence for most of the way back. I had to fight not to speed as well. I could feel the adrenaline pumping through me, and I also wanted to get back to the safety of the dorm.

It wasn't just H3RO that lived in the dorm, so security was much tighter there, and it was also, somehow, unknown to the outside world. Although there was an entrance to the underground parking, the front of the building looked more like an office block.

"Go on up," I told them after I had parked up.

"Are you OK?" Minhyuk asked me.

"Me?" I asked, surprised. "I'm fine. They were swarming the minibus to see you. Are you OK?"

"It was kind of terrifying," he admitted.

I glanced back at the others. Kyun still looked pale. Jun wasn't his usual cheerful self, and I was sure Nate's eyes hadn't moved from the back of my head since we had left the studio (I'd caught him watching me every time I'd looked in the rearview mirror). "You have a free schedule this afternoon," I told them all brightly. "Go up and chill out. We'll order in food later and watch a movie, or something. We have an early call tomorrow and a packed day, so make the most of it."

"What about you?" Nate demanded.

"I am going to check the minibus, and then I'm going to go to the police station to make my statement,"

I told him. "I'll join you guys later."

"I'm coming with you," Tae declared.

"You are absolutely not," I shot back at him, much to his surprise. "Your face is noticeable. I am not having you walking into a police station because I do not want to have to deal with a bunch of bullshit news articles that will be associated with it. Plus, given everything that has just happened, I would rather you just go in and keep your heads down so we don't have a repeat performance."

Tae shot me a look, then opened the door, disappearing into the dorms. I sighed and got out myself, although I occupied myself with examining the minibus. I hadn't been exaggerating earlier. The minibus really was 'well loved' with dints and chips all over. As far as I could tell, there was nothing new.

"Are you sure you don't want company?"

I turned and found Nate watching me. I gave him a soft smile but shook my head. "I don't know how long I'll be gone," I told him. "Hopefully, not long. Please just go in and relax."

"I'm not sure if I can relax while you're out there," Nate muttered.

I rolled my eyes. "I'm your manager. No one cares about me."

"I do," he shrugged, though his eyes met mine with a heated stare.

"That's not what I meant," I said, quietly.

He stepped forward, wrapping his arms around me. I closed my eyes and breathed him in, feeling completely secure in his embrace. "Be careful," he murmured, kissing my forehead.

I sighed, then stepped away. "I'm just going to the

police station," I assured him. "I'll be back soon."

제7 장

H3RO

Stop Stop It

I was only in the police station for a couple of hours and most of that was spent waiting for the officer to become available to take my statement. He'd been very professional about it however pointed out that he had been around many idols over the years and with popularity like this, it would be wise to have additional security with us.

He was right, and I had been thinking of my options while I had been waiting. Instead of returning to the dorm, I went to the office. Specifically, Lee Sejin's office. He looked as thrilled to see me as a child did in a dentist's waiting room … fine by me. The treatment H3RO was receiving was like a giant cavity and I was set on filling it.

"What do you want?" he asked, although his tone told me he didn't really care why I was there, just that my mere presence was causing an irritation. Good.

"Stop blocking me with my decisions," I told him.

He glanced over at me and sneered. "Stop making stupid decisions."

"Requesting additional security is not a stupid

decision, Sejin. It's a smart one."

Sejin rolled his eyes. "Have you considered acting? You'd be perfect for a melodrama."

"I am not being melodramatic," I said, making sure I kept my cool, even though he was already winding me up. "Do you know where I've been all afternoon?"

"I'm guessing booking a one-way ticket back to Chicago is too much to ask for?" he asked with a sickly-sweet smile.

I scowled at him, folding my arms under my breasts. "The police station, Sejin. I've been at the police station."

Sejin regarded me with suspicion. "Why?"

"Because when we tried to leave the *Seoul Nights* recording, we were surrounded by fans."

Sejin choked back a laugh. "H3RO have fans?"

"We got a number one single, dickhead," I snapped at him. "I think it's safe to say that H3RO have fans."

"Huh," he shrugged, sitting back in his chair. "I didn't see that one coming."

"No, you wouldn't," I agreed, with a growl. "Because you constantly have low expectations when it comes to H3RO, even when they're clearly exceeding any and all expectations you have."

Sejin regarded me with a blank expression. "You thought I had expectations for them?" With a growl, I yanked a piece of paper from my handbag, walking over and slammed it on his desk. I took a sliver of satisfaction from the look of fear that appeared at that. "What is this?" he demanded.

"A list of names that the police got from the incident," I informed him. The police officer had provided me with the list as I left, both a printed copy and an emailed copy.

"What do you expect me to do with that?" he asked, picking it up at the very edge of the page like I had coated it with poison … damn, it was too late to do that now …

"You?" I shrugged. "I expect you to do fuck all with it, like you continue to do with H3RO. What I hope you would do is pass it on to the security team, so we can monitor these names and make sure they don't end up causing further problems in the future. Like I know you do with Onyx and Cupcake."

I knew full well that Black Hearts and Frosting, the respective fandoms, were generally very well behaved and supportive of their beloved groups, but they had had the occasional weird fan in there. Youngbin, Onyx's leader and Bella, Cupcake's lead vocalist, had both had sasaeng. At least in Youngbin's case, his was international.

"Atlantis has a policy, where you are building up cases for the crazier Onyx and Cupcake fans, to protect their members. You should be doing the same for H3RO." I didn't bother waiting for a response. There was no point. Instead, I left the office and made my way to the office of the only person who had more power than Sejin.

This time, I'd called ahead to schedule an appointment with Lee Woojin.

"Holly," he greeted me, warmly. He gestured that I should sit.

Instead, I walked over to his desk and put my hands on my hips as I stared down at him. "Why am I here?"

He looked up at me in confusion. "You made this appointment, did you not?"

"No," I said, with a brusque shake of my head. "Why am I in Korea? Why did you bring me to Atlantis?"

"Do you know why I created Atlantis?" he asked me.

My eyes widened. "Really?"

"When I was at school, my three best friends started a band. They were signed to an agency and within six months of their debut, were one of the biggest selling groups that year," he explained before I could tell him I really couldn't care. "By the end of the year, one of them was dead, and another in a coma."

I sank into the chair which had been previously offered, my mouth falling open. "What happened?"

Woojin pointed to a something behind me. I turned in my seat. In the center of the wall was a two-meter squared framed image of a band that looked like they could easily have debuted in the early seventies. "K-pop wasn't the same as it is now, but music still existed."

I turned back to him. I wasn't sure how this was relevant to me, but I didn't think it was completely appropriate to tell him that. "I'm sorry about your friends," I told him.

"I ended up creating Atlantis for Moon Cheolmin."

I recognized that name. He was a, now retired, actor who had been on the Atlantis Entertainment roster. I glanced back over my shoulder. The picture was very old compared to the last image I'd seen of Moon Cheolmin, but I was certain he was the bass guitarist in the photograph.

"If I'd have had my way, I would have made sure Moon Cheolmin never returned to the idol world at all. I hate it. But that was what he wanted, so I wanted to create a company which would find and nurture its artists. I took a loan from my father, started the company, and bought his contract out."

I snorted loudly at that statement.

"I did," Lee Woojin said with a small frown. "And I think it was like that to start with. There's a reason why we have such a high number of individuals auditioning for our company."

I gave him a look of disbelief. "If this is what you call nurturing, I'm going to guess that there's a very different meaning in Korean than there is in English."

"It may be said differently, but the meaning is the same. And that is partly why I want you here. Since Sejin started working here, we climbed up to be the number four company in South Korea. The K-Pop industry is highly lucrative. He has an excellent business head on him and he knows what is needed to be done to keep us there." I snorted again, rolling my eyes. "But therein lies the problem. His nurturing side is somewhat lacking."

"Somewhat?" I scoffed. "I've heard some understatements recently, but that one has to top them all."

"That's why I need you. To balance him out."

I stared at the man in front of me in disbelief. "Balance him out?" I repeated. "You need a saint to do that, and I'm not one of those."

"If you've got half the genes of your mother, you are," he told me.

I stood up abruptly. "What's the other part?" I

demanded.

"The other part?"

I nodded. "You said me being here was in part, to balance that asshole half-brother out. What's the other part?"

"You are my daughter," he said, simply.

"If you want me to balance Lee Sejin out," I said, choosing to ignore that statement, "You need to give me more power. I accept that I might not know much about this industry, and it's a learning curve where I will make mistakes, but what I'm doing, I'm doing with the absolute best interest of H3RO."

"I understand," he nodded.

"That means when I request security, I get it. And when I start working on their next comeback, I have a budget," I continued. "I appreciate that until now H3RO haven't been fulfilling their potential, but I think a large part of that has been at the fault of Atlantis, so stop holding them back, and instead, protect and support them. If nothing else, the very bottom line is that they are making this company money: they are an asset. If you want them to keep making money, you need to look after them. You need to allow me to look after them."

"I think you are a good fit for H3RO," Woojin told me. "I remember being at all their auditions, and I even put that group together. You see them as individuals as well as a group."

Hearing him compliment me was weird, so I left him. I had hopefully gotten what I had gone to see him for, although with a whole other pile of *what the fuck was that* to go along with it.

H3RO

I was exhausted. I had spent the day running on adrenaline, moving from one thing to another. After a very lengthy conversation with the security team, they had agreed (once Lee Woojin had called down) to assess the security situation with H3RO. They'd also informed me that they would check the names I'd provided them to make sure there wasn't a history of weird behavior there, and would also add them to their database—just in case.

Maybe I was overreacting, but I had been terrified. I walked to my office, wanting to collect my thoughts before I went back to the dorm. On my way, I walked straight into someone. "I'm sorry," I apologized, before realizing it was my other half-brother.

"Are you OK?" Seungjin asked, peering down at me.

I don't know why, but at that moment I knew I was going to cry. I nodded, then hurried away, abandoning him before I burst into tears on him.

In the safety of my office, I sank into the chair behind the desk, kicking off my shoes, and turned to face the window. I then stopped fighting the tears. I think, more than anything, it was the sense of relief that *finally*, I was getting Atlantis to listen to me and look after H3RO.

It wasn't a proper crying session, so much as the frustration and adrenaline leaving me in tear format. Regardless, it felt cathartic. I reached for my purse, pulling out my iPad, wanting to check the schedule for tomorrow so I could send it on to security before heading back to the dorm. We had two shows—one very early, and one very late. It was going to be a long day.

I hit send, then slipped the device back into my purse. I stood, ready to go home, but was distracted by the view. Instead, I sat back down, this time on the desk, my feet on the chair, and stared out the window. The sun was starting to set and it was washing Seoul with a warm orange color. It was pretty. The view from the office, while not as impressive as Sejin's 180-degree view, was still spectacular.

There was a knock at the door. I ignored it. I was not in the mood to talk to anyone and play nice. The person on the other side of the door didn't get the hint and walked in, shutting the door behind them.

For some reason, I was fully expecting it to be Sejin ready for round two, especially as I had gone to see Woojin and the security team. I looked over my shoulder, ready to tell him to get lost, but stopped when I saw Jun standing there. "Jun?" Forgetting to act ladylike and slip down off the desk, I swirled around and lowered my bare feet on the opposite side. By the time I had done this, Jun was already in front of me.

"Seungjin messaged me."

"I …" I frowned. "You have a phone?"

Jun shook his head. "He went via the group account on Instagram. Said you were upset."

"I'm not upset," I sighed.

"Then why are you sat all alone in this office?"

I laughed. "Jun, this is *my* office. Where I work … which is what I've been doing."

"It looked like you were staring out the window, plotting murder, to me."

"That might also be accurate," I conceded. I gave him a small smile. I had been expecting him to move back but he didn't and getting off the desk had only closed the gap between us. I cleared my throat. "But it's time to go back to the dorm now."

"Not yet," Jun whispered.

I glanced up at him, then regretted it as I got caught up in a smolder. Uh-oh.

"I would like to have some time with you by myself before I have to share you with the others," he continued, still whispering, his voice husky.

Uber uh-oh … I cleared my throat. "We've spent a lot of time together over the last couple of weeks," I quickly pointed out.

"Not just us two." He took three steps forward. I took two steps back and my butt hit my desk. His hands grabbed the edge of the desk, either side of me. Slowly, he started to lower his head, bringing his lips towards mine.

"Anyone could walk in," I whispered, surprised I couldn't make the words louder.

"I locked the door behind me." His eyes, unblinking, never left mine. His lips were so close I was breathing in the warm air he was breathing out. They just hovered there, like he was waiting for me to make that final move.

"We should probably talk," I muttered. Jun, Nate, Dante, Tae … I wasn't choosing one over the other at this point, but I figured it was only fair he should know. And then I stopped myself.

"Stop over thinking things," he said, leaning in closer—I didn't realize it was possible to get closer at this point, but he did.

"No, you need to know," I said, quietly.

"Maybe I already do," he said. My eyes widened as he abruptly closed the gap with more force than was necessary. His lips claimed mine while his hands circled around my back and jerked me to him. My hands shot out to steady myself, landing on his chest. He started sucking at my lower lip and when he started nibbling at it, my hands fisted around his hoodie, pulling him as close to me as I could get him, opening my mouth and inviting him in.

제8 장

H3R오

Power

His tongue darted in, and he kissed me hard, our teeth occasionally knocking each other until we fell into a fast, hard rhythm. When I started to pull away, his teeth caught my lower lip and pulled me closer. It was a sharp bite of pain, but I found myself moaning in pleasure from it. I could feel Jun's mouth curl up in a smile at that.

His hands seized my waist and he lifted me so I was sitting on the edge of my desk. He began pushing his knees between mine, and I parted before I could stop to think about what I was doing. His hands started moving upwards, skimming over my breasts.

Lost in a haze of lust as I kissed him, I didn't realize what he was doing until the blouse had been ripped open. I jerked my head back at the sound of the buttons popping off. "Jun!" I exclaimed.

"It was getting in the way of these," he growled, his eyes focused on my breasts. He glanced up at me, and the look he gave me sent swarms of butterflies pounding in my chest. Or maybe that was my heart. I glanced down, certain I would be able to see it pounding out of my ribcage.

He let out an incoherent growl as he ran a hand over my breasts. His touch had heat shooting everywhere, making my sensitive areas throb. I arched back, sticking my breasts out for him. There was another incoherent sentence and then he lowered his head, his tongue darting between my cleavage.

Then, he clamped his mouth around one of my nipples sucking it through the thin satin of my bra. While one hand supported my back, holding me in place, the other took ahold of my other nipple, rolling the hard bud between his fingers.

I moaned, loudly, my hands locking around his hair, holding him in place. He sucked harder. As my moan grew louder, his other hand pinched at my other nipple, pulling and twisting. "Oh, *hell!*" I cried. The hot mouth and the pain—the combination was exquisite torture.

His mouth released me, but before I could complain, he had swapped, his tongue now soothing the sweet pain his hand had left behind. The hand on my back left me, moving to my free nipple. This one slipped down below the cup and I gasped at the touch of his fingertips on me before they started pinching and twisting my nipple again.

My hands let go of Jun's hair, flying backwards to keep myself upright. Jun's free hand shot around me, this time pulling me to him. I could feel him. He was hard, pressing up against me, but with his head and his hands where they were, I couldn't get at him.

I tried to reach down, but Jun's hand left my breast and batted my hand away. Then it was back on my nipple, giving me an extra hard pinch. "Fuck that,"

I grunted at him. My hands went straight back to his jeans, unbuttoning them, then tugging the zip down. I reached inside, pulling him free and wrapping my hand around him as his hands twisted my nipple once more. His mouth released my other nipple with a hiss.

The other breast was released from his fingers as he wrapped his hand around mine, starting to move it up and down, along his cock. Although I wanted his mouth and hands back on me, the knowledge I was now the one in control was even hotter. I brought my hand to his tip, running a thumb over it and he released another hiss, his forehead dropping forward against my chest. "Fuck, Holly," he grunted into my breasts.

I moved his hand away, then increased the pace. His hands moved to the desk, gripping at the wood like he needed to hold himself upright.

I liked that.

He was breathing heavily against my chest, his mouth moving every so often to nip at my nipples. The power over him was heady, and I realized that I could have my revenge—every time he looked at me with his *I know how to make you moan* look, I would return it with my own.

Without losing my pace, I shuffled off the desk. When Jun looked up at me with questioning eyes, I gave him my own smirk and started sinking to my knees. His hands wrapped around my shoulders, half holding me in place. "Holly," he hissed.

I rubbed my thumb around the tip of his cock again and he swore under his breath, his hands going back to the table. I continued my descent and then moved my hand back down so I could replace my thumb with my tongue. That rewarded me with a groan of pleasure.

I took him in my mouth, moving my head in time with my hands. His hands went to my hair, twisting it through his fingers. I could sense him staring at me, and I glanced up. I was right. His dark eyes, filled with heat and lust, were fixed on me. "Holly," he moaned, the sound urging me on. I could taste him on my tongue.

I started increasing my pace, alternating the pressure from my hand with my mouth. "Holly," he moaned again, sounding more desperate this time. His hands gripped gently at my head as he tried to pull me away. With my other hand, I batted him away, keeping my control. "Holly," he tried again.

I looked up at him, briefly catching his eye, noting the look of surprise, then he swore. His body went rigid and then his orgasm filled my mouth. I didn't stop my caress until he had nothing left to give me.

"Holly," he murmured when I finally released him. He was trying to catch his breath as he helped me to my feet. "You didn't have to do that."

"I'm aware," I agreed as I leaned back against the desk.

I started trying to correct my clothing, but Jun's hands grabbed mine, holding them to my side. "I hadn't finished with these," he declared, lowering his head back to my breasts.

And then there was a knock at the door as someone wrapped at the door. "Miss Holly?" someone called.

"Are you kidding me?" I muttered.

"I have a delivery for you," the voice called again.

Jun stopped what he was doing, hurriedly pulling his hoody off, giving it to me. By the time I had pulled it over my head to hide the ripped blouse, he was already sitting on one of the couches in the office, an arm over the back, acting as though he hadn't just orgasmed in the middle of my office.

"Miss Holly!" the knocking continued. "Are you alright?"

I jumped off the desk, smoothing my hair as I hurried over to the door. I unlocked it and found an Atlantis employee I vaguely recognized staring at me, his eyes wide with concern. "I'm OK," I assured him, praying my face wasn't as red and flustered as it felt.

"You have mail," he said, stepping back to reveal the stack of boxes.

"What are all of those?" I asked, my eyes growing wide.

"This is the fan mail for H3RO. Lee Sejin said it should be brought to you," the man explained. I stepped back to allow them to be wheeled in, then closed the door behind him.

Jun was already investigating by the time I walked over. There were fourteen large boxes, each full of letters and small packages. Jun had picked up a letter and opened it, reading it. He grinned then looked over at me. "Noona, we have fan mail."

"You've never had any?" I asked, surprised.

Jun slowly shook his head, and then started digging through another box. He plucked out a packet and quickly unwrapped it, revealing a box of designer boxers. "I got sent underwear!" he yelled. "Yes!"

I tilted my head and caught the name on the wrapping. "Jun, they were addressed to Minhyuk."

Jun laughed, shrugging. "Finder's keepers!"

I leaned over, snatching the items from him and

putting them back in the box. "Enough," I chided him.

"But *nooooooooona,*" he whined.

"Grab a box," I instructed, ignoring his pout. "We'll take some back to the dorm and let everyone open them." I picked one up, and watched as Jun decided to pick up three. "Really?" I asked. He couldn't even see from behind the stack.

"I am trying to impress you with my manliness," he declared.

I laughed. "Are you sure? I walked here."

Jun set the boxes back down, then picked up two. This time I could see his face. "I could manage three," He informed me, matter of factly. "I just didn't want to show up Dante when I walked in the dorm."

"Of course," I agreed, with a light chuckle.

We made our way downstairs and, at my insistence, out the back entrance. There were usually fans lurking around the front, and after our earlier encounter, I wasn't in the mood for a going through the same thing again. "What do you want to eat?" I asked as we walked back. "I promised food earlier."

"Pizza. Always pizza," Jun grinned.

"We might need to put that to a vote," I sighed. I'd noticed that: how he managed to eat so much pizza and have a figure like he did was beyond me.

"Noona?"

I blinked and looked over at him. "Huh?" I hadn't realized he had been saying anything.

"I said, are you really OK?"

"Why wouldn't I be?" I asked.

"I mean from the incident in the bus earlier. You looked pretty shaken up," he elaborated.

"I didn't care for that, and I'm in no hurry for a

repeat performance, but I'm OK," I assured him. "I guess I didn't realize how scary being an idol could be. But it *shouldn't* happen again," I added. "I've spoken to the security team. We'll have security with us next time."

We were halfway home when it happened.

For the second time, something went hurtling towards me. I caught sight of it from the corner of my eye and managed to turn my head to stop it hitting me in the face, but carrying the box, I couldn't put my hands up in time and stop it hitting me altogether.

I screamed as something exploded just behind my ear. Then I dropped the box I was carrying, yelling out in pain once more as the corner landed on my foot.

"Holly!" Jun cried, all but throwing his boxes to the ground as he pulled me back, out of the middle of the sidewalk, trying to work out what had happened.

"It's an egg," I told him through gritted teeth. I wasn't sure if it was where it had hit, or if it had been thrown harder this time, but it hurt. As did my foot.

Jun turned to me, tilting my head so he could examine it. "I think it's just—oh, wow!" he exclaimed, stepping back and holding his nose.

Before I could think about what I was doing, I poked my fingers in it. As I brought my fingers around to look at it, I realized why Jun had reacted as he had. "It's rotten!" I exclaimed, the smell turning my stomach. "Oh, I'm going to be sick," I murmured. That was it— once I smelled it, I couldn't un-smell it.

"Let's get back to the dorm," Jun murmured.

I nodded, bending down to scoop up the dropped box, wincing as my hair, and the egg, fell in my face. I took a step forward, then stopped, biting my lip so I wouldn't cry out in pain as Jun was distracted by collecting his discarded boxes.

It didn't work. He set them straight back down, then pulled mine from my hand. "You're injured," he stated.

"It's my foot," I admitted. I was wearing heels with no upper covering. The box had been dropped from a height and was heavy. Somehow my ankle hadn't buckled under me, but putting weight on it to walk was painful.

Jun crouched down and gently prodded it. "Ow!" I yelped, jerking my foot out of the way. I of course lost my balance and went tumbling straight into him.

"I should have known you like to be on top," Jun told me cheekily.

I peered down at him, trying not to move incase my hair fell forward onto him. I closed my eyes and sighed. "This is not a good day."

"It had its highlights," Jun chuckled. He lifted me up, placing me to his side before rolling over to crouch in front of me. "Stay there," he said, pulling the hood up and over my hair.

"The egg!" I cried as it was smeared across the side of my face and the inside of his hood.

"Necessary evil," he muttered.

Before I could ask him what he was doing, he had gathered up all three boxes and disappeared into the small convenience store we'd been in front of. He reappeared moments later, empty handed. "What did you do with those?" I asked him.

"Can't carry everything," he responded. Then he leaned down and scooped me up in his arms.

"Jun," I started to object.

He shook his head. "I can't carry you on my back

with that skirt on."

"I was going to point out that if we walked slowly, I could manage that," I corrected him as he hurried down the street to the dorm.

"Yeah, but you stink," Jun retorted.

"Your chat-up lines are getting better," I muttered, dryly. Unfortunately, he was right. The smell of the rotten egg was still turning my stomach.

We burst into the dorm the door flying open. "Jun, is that necessary?" Tae scolded him. He stopped when he realized I was in the maknae's arms. "What happened?"

He hurried over, Minhyuk with him. "What the *hell* is that smell?" Minhyuk cried, almost going green as he covered his mouth and took a step back.

"Someone threw an egg again," Jun replied for me. "This one was rotten."

"It's disgusting," Dante cried from the other side of the room.

"Try having it in your hair!" I yelled back at him, then Jun was carrying me to the bathroom. Tae and Minhyuk were right behind me, the former bringing a chair with him.

A flash of déjà vu flashed through me as I was set down on a chair with my back to the sink. I closed my eyes, somehow managing to forget about the egg as I dropped my head forward into my hands. And then the green and black tinged raw egg was all over my hands.

That was it—I couldn't take it anymore. I lunged at the toilet bowl and threw up the little I had in my stomach. "What's going on?" I heard Nate from the doorway. "What's wrong with Holly?"

"Out!" I heard Minhyuk suddenly order.

Technically, Minhyuk fell under the bracket of the maknae line, but I glanced up to see him ushering his leader from the bathroom. He did manage it with a lot more respect than he showed Jun, literally shoving him out of the door.

"I'm covered in it too!" Jun cried.

"Do you plan on showering with Holly?" Minhyuk demanded.

I could see Jun's eyes light up, then he was rewarded with a smack to the back of the head by Dante. "Use the kitchen or go downstairs and use the studio bathrooms," Minhyuk snapped, slamming the door in their faces.

제9장

H3R오

Don't Touch My Girl

There was a knock at the door and Minhyuk whipped it open. "What?"

"For Holly," I heard Dante.

"Thank you," Minhyuk responded. He shut the door more gently this time.

"Oh, you don't need to witness this," I groaned, turning my head back to the bowl.

"You're a mess," Minhyuk pointed out, moving over so he could crouch down beside me. "That really needs washing out and that's the last thing you need turning to scrambled egg."

He was right about that. I pulled back and Minhyuk reached over, scraping the hair from my face. "What are you doing?"

"I have a strong stomach," he said.

"You're green," I retorted.

"Then let's get you cleaned up quickly," he shrugged. "We need to start by getting that hoodie off you." He bit his lip, suddenly going embarrassed.

"I can do this by myself if you prefer," I offered, gently.

"No, you can't," Minhyuk sighed. "I just … do you mind?" I shook my head. "OK, one thing at a time. Let's see if we can get this off without it going everywhere."

"That would be good," I agreed.

Minhyuk grabbed at the cuff of my sleeve, pulling my arm loose, then reached for the other. Once both were free, using the hood, he tugged the hoodie off. That felt marginally better.

Until I realized he was staring at me in shock. I glanced down and caught a glance of myself. OK … his reaction was understandable. My blouse, torn by Jun earlier, was hanging open, exposing my bra. From how I'd been hugging the toilet bowl, my skirt had ridden up too. "There's an explanation," I muttered.

"Let's deal with one thing at a time," he said. He pulled a face, looking awkward. "Holly, it's on your blouse too."

I was beyond embarrassed now, pulling the blouse off. Minhyuk reached over and balled it up in the hoodie. He hurried over to the door, poked it open and shoved the offending clothing into the hallway. "Someone throw these out!" he called, before shutting the door.

He made his way back to me and offered me something—a bottle of water and some painkillers. "Thank you," I murmured, assuming this was what Dante had given him. I took a mouthful of water, swilling it around my mouth, then spat it out into the toilet. I did it a couple of times until my mouth felt a little cleaner, but the nausea remained. I could still smell the egg. I took the painkiller with a sigh. My head was pounding now. My foot was also throbbing.

"I'll wash your hair, and then you can have a shower," Minhyuk said. He reached down to help me up. I flushed the toilet then accepted his help, straightening my skirt before settling down in the chair. Minhyuk glanced down at me, then quickly looked away. He reached over for a towel, then carefully draped it over me.

"Thank you," I muttered, holding the towel too me.

Behind me, Minhyuk set the water running, then lowered me back. "I would have thought that after Atlantis announced you are our manager, that this wouldn't happen again."

I blinked, staring up at his upside-down head in surprise. "You think this was aimed at me?"

"You don't?"

"I ..." I frowned. Both times I had been with Jun. I had, for some reason, thought this was because it was aimed at him. I was a nobody. Why would anyone throw anything at me?

But, thinking about it, someone throwing an egg at Jun made less sense. He was an idol and he had fans. The first time, the thrower had even told me to stay away from him. This second time, I was with him again. If it was a fan, it would make more sense that they were jealous I was with them. "Oh," I mumbled. "That does make more sense."

Minhyuk rubbed some shampoo in my hair, then allowed it to sit while he grabbed a wash cloth and wiped at the side of my head and neck. "You'll need a shower to remove it completely, but this will help."

It did—the smell was slowly disappearing down the sink.

"Who does that though?" I asked, more to myself than to Minhyuk.

"I've heard of ARMY and EXO-Ls getting a little possessive over their favorite members," Minhyuk said, thoughtfully. "Though I've never heard of them attacking staff."

"Yes, well the world knows what their managers look like, and knows that they are men." I frowned. "Not that that makes this right."

Minhyuk rinsed off my hair, then squeezed the excess water off, before helping me upright. "I think you're safe to shower now."

"Thank you, Minhyuk-ah," I said, gratefully. I waited for him to leave the bathroom, and then set the shower running. Under the hot water, I tried to relax, but the realization that someone had intentionally thrown those eggs at me had sent a chill down my spine that I couldn't shake.

I stared down at my foot and the big bruise that was forming. "Rather me than Jun," I said, quietly.

I quickly showered, and then wrapped myself in a towel to limp as quickly as I could with a painful foot over to my room where I towel-dried my hair. I wrapped it up into a messy bun on the top of my head. By the time I was dressed in some pajamas, the painkillers had kicked in. My appetite had yet to reappear though.

I made my way back to the living area and found my eyes watering at the overwhelming smell of man scent. Which man scent, I wasn't sure: I had a hunch that all six of them had gone into their collections and started spraying everything they owned.

And I could still smell the lingering decay of that

egg.

"Next time, we're hosing you off on the roof," Nate joked as I joined them.

"Oh guys, this is horrific," I said, pulling a face. Heat be damned, I was opening a window.

I was hobbling over when I was scooped up off my feet, despite my squeals, by Jun. "What are you doing?" I protested as he moved me over to the couch.

"Your foot," he said, pointing at the offending limb after he had set me down.

"Do we need to take you to the hospital?" Tae asked, moving over to examine my foot.

"It's a bruise, not a break!" I hollered at them. "It will be fine in the morning—and if you're going to stop me walking around, could someone please open a window so we can get some fresh air in here?"

"They only open a crack," Minhyuk said, apologetically as he moved over to fulfil my request.

"If you open one of the bedroom windows, or the door, it will at least get a breeze running through," I suggested. Something was better than nothing. My eyes fell on Dante who was now walking over with a first aid kit. I arched an eyebrow. "Dante, what do you plan on doing with that?"

He pointed at my foot.

"It's a *bruise*," I said again, pulling my foot out of Tae's hands and crossing my legs so I could curl it up underneath me. Then I started laughing. The day was one absurd mess.

Dante turned to Tae with a bewildered look. "Did you break her?"

"Someone order food," I said, trying to stop myself from laughing as Tae looked at Jun with a confused expression.

"Pizza!" Jun yelled as both Kyun and Nate groaned.

Somehow the pizza won out, although I declined from ordering one for myself. Instead, I focused on the new addition to the room: the three boxes of fan mail. Jun must have been to collect them. I got up to go over to them but was pushed firmly back down by Tae. "Nope," he said. "Tonight, you rest."

I sighed and pointed at the boxes. "That's what I dropped on my foot," I explained. "It's your fan mail."

"We have fan mail?" Kyun asked, his eyes wide as he looked from me to the boxes.

I nodded, fighting to keep the anger from my face. I was going to murder Lee Sejin in his sleep. "It's only a small selection. I'd walked to the office, otherwise I would have loaded the van up with them and brought them all back. Go investigate!" I encouraged them.

H3RO, minus Tae, descended on the boxes like a pack of lions on a kill. I glanced up at Tae and looked at him questioningly. "I think it would be a good idea if you didn't walk to the office anymore," he said, quietly, sitting down beside me.

"It's just down the street," I shrugged. "Getting the car out, driving there, and parking up again would take way longer than it would to just walk it. Plus, I like the exercise."

"Use the gym," Tae said, shortly.

"And the fresh air," I added, narrowing my eyes.

"Go sit on the roof." He scowled back at me.

"It's just an egg," I said, slowly.

"This time it's just an egg," he said. "What about next time?"

I sighed. "Fine." I had no intention of driving to the office. What I was going to do was report this matter to security and the police and get them to investigate. "Why don't you go open something before Jun claims it all?" I suggested, pointing at the pile of letters. Someone had made the decision to empty all three boxes into one pile in the middle of the floor, and the five of them were sat around reading the letters like it was Christmas.

He didn't look thrilled with me, but Tae did as I suggested and joined the others. He quickly forgot his irritation as he started opening his own mail.

I sank back into the sofa and stretched out, watching them, a smile on my face. It was great to be able to see this. I caught snippets of conversation as they read parts of the letters out to each other.

"Holly has letters too!" Jun cried.

I looked at him, startled. "Huh?"

He bounded over with three letters. "Look!"

I took them off him: sure enough, I did. Curious, I opened the first one. "What does it say?" Nate asked.

I quickly read it, before laughing. "It's thanking me for helping you guys with your comeback."

"Why are you laughing?" Minhyuk asked, tilting his head at me.

I held the letter up. "Thank you for looking after H3RO," I read. "And I don't know if the video had anything to do with you; but thank you for allowing Dante to grace the world with his abs, because *damn*. Please note I will be sending you my funeral expense separately, because those abs killed me."

Nate dropped his head into his hand with a groan. "Why?"

Dante, leaped to his feet, grinning like the Cheshire Cat, and pulled his top up. "These abs?" he asked, doing a body roll.

"He's going to be insufferable now," Jun added, earning himself a clip to the back of the head from Dante.

I cleared my throat. "All my love, Ryan."

Jun burst out laughing, but Dante cocked his head at me, dropping his shirt. "Ryan is a guy's name?" I nodded. Dante frowned some more, and then he shrugged. In one movement, he pulled his t-shirt over his head. "If Ryan can appreciate this masterpiece, why can't you?" he demanded of his group, flexing his muscles at them.

"Probably because of the mouth that's attached to it?" Tae suggested.

Dante whirled around, ready to clip him, then stopped when he realized it had been Tae, and not Jun who was beside him who had said that. Then he pulled a face at his leader. "I don't see Holly having a problem with this mouth."

I was going to murder him.

Although I was dying on the inside, I fixed him an innocent stare. "It's not the mouth that's the problem—it's the ego."

"Burn!" Jun cried, this time earning the smack upside his head.

I shook my head, chuckling to myself as my phone bleeped to tell me the pizza was here. "The pizza is downstairs," I announced.

"Jun will go," Tae decided, fixing the maknae a stare. Jun just shrugged and did as instructed.

I settled back to read the other letters. The second

was a much sweeter version of the first, thanking me for my hard work. I had no idea why, really—it was H3RO doing it all, not me.

The third one was different.

Stay away from H3RO.

That was all it said, but it was enough to send a chill down my spine. I glanced over at the group. They were still preoccupied with their own letters. I folded this one back up and put it back in the envelope. That was going to Atlantis.

I looked up again, this time my attention fell on Kyun. He wasn't watching me, absorbed in his own letter, but he looked upset. Before I could say anything, Jun chose that moment to return to the dorm, his arms laden with pizza boxes.

While the group stood up to claim their pizzas, Kyun got up, shoving the letter into his pocket. "I'm not hungry," he muttered, before disappearing down the hallway to his bedroom. I shot Tae a look. He shrugged at me, then disappeared after his friend.

Nate came and joined me on the couch, offering me a slice of pizza. I turned my nose up at it. "Only a heathen puts pineapple on a pizza," I declared, pushing the Hawaiian pizza back to him in disgust.

"Have you seen what Jun ordered?" Nate asked in disbelief. "And it was good enough for the Hawaiians."

"You do know it was created by a Greek guy in Canada, right?" I asked.

Nate's mouth fell open. "What?"

제10 장

H3RO

Sorry For My English

I slammed my hand down on my alarm, cursing its existence. The early morning roll call for the next show meant we had to be up at 3am to get to the studio and H3RO into makeup.

This was the part of the whole thing I didn't like. It wasn't that I was the sort to stay in bed all day, but 3am was not a normal time to be getting up. I got out of bed, and got dressed, shivering in the cold morning air. Then I set about waking the others up. Unsurprisingly, Jun was the worst one to wake up. Jun loved his sleep. Luckily, his roommate, Nate was the opposite. He was also not quiet when he got up either, making sure the radio and the overhead lights were on.

Dante was usually the first up as he was the one who would be in the bathroom first. Honestly, I had no idea how the six of them had managed to share a bathroom without killing each other. That was probably why the bathroom didn't have a working lock. I'd worked that out the hard way … at the same time I discovered that Dante didn't sleep with clothes on, nor did he have an issue walking around naked.

Thankfully, although my foot was now sporting a wicked looking bruise, and it was tender to touch, I was able to walk without too much trouble. Considering the busy schedule, I was grateful.

We left the dorm early, and with little traffic on the road at that time in the morning, the drive was smooth. It was also the first time we had security. Atlantis had provided us with a second minibus, albeit one which was still as tired looking as our usual one, but it meant that H3RO could spread out over the two vehicles, and the two drivers were from the security team.

I sat behind the driver, providing the directions, while Tae and Minhyuk headed to the back and promptly went back to sleep. It took me a while to realize that Kyun, who was sitting beside me, wasn't asleep. "Are you OK?" I asked him, quietly.

"Yes," he responded, shortly.

I chewed at my lip, wondering if I should press it. Kyun was the quietest of the group, and often seemed the grumpiest, even beating Tae. Tae, although quiet, was more serious than moody, and usually spending the time silently checking up on his group.

This wasn't the first time I'd worried about Kyun. Back when they were preparing for the comeback, he'd been off his meals, but as he'd pointed out, he was just trying to get back in shape and didn't need to eat all the high carb food Minhyuk kept preparing. Which would have made sense if he wasn't eating ramyun all the time.

I tried to study him as best I could, without staring too hard at him. He looked tired, but it was nearly four in the morning, and I wasn't looking the freshest, so I couldn't really pass judgement on that. But he did look thinner. I didn't want to compare him to one of the others. None of them had the same height or body shape, but he didn't look as healthy as they did. Maybe he was coming down with something?

"I'm fine," he huffed again, wrapping his jacket more tightly around him, and angling his body towards the window and away from me. I sighed. So much for being discreet. Evidently, it was best not to press it. I'd check with Tae later and just make sure there wasn't anything to worry about.

We finally made it to the studio and it was early enough that only a handful of the die-hard fans were there. None, I noted, were the same ones who had surrounded the minibus from the previous day.

H3RO spent some time saying hello, then went inside for their hair and makeup. The show was a new one. With K-Pop growing in popularity, more shows were popping up aimed at the international fans. This one was aimed at the US audience, hence the early time. It was also one with two Korean-American hosts—one of which was Bella Hong from Atlantis Entertainment's girl group, Cupcake.

The aim of the show was simple. They would perform a non-title track, then they would sit while the hosts read through a list of questions in both Korean and English that had been sent in via various SNS sites. If the guests could answer in English, they would, and if not, the hosts would translate. Then, at the end, they would perform the title track.

It was performed in front of a small live audience, one where international fans were given first choice on seats, as well as via online two-way streaming. Both were given the opportunity to question the guests live.

It wasn't the first show of its type, but it was getting a lot of viewers from around the world.

Normally, I didn't really watch the shows when H3RO made an appearance. I hung around only paying half of my attention. They were usually asked the same questions and I trusted them to get on with it, however, I was usually multitasking with Atlantis related work (the company was massive, and although I was currently managing H3RO, I wanted to know exactly what else this company did).

Today, as it was so early, my devices stayed in my bag. Naturally, Nate was taking the lead with the English-speaking parts, although Dante was also quite fluent. Tae and Minhyuk could manage simple answers, and Jun was being entertaining with his one word (sometimes) appropriate answers. Just as he was in person, he continued to be sarcastic and dry. I had a feeling he would excel as an MC given the chance. Then Nate got up and joined the hosts, and I decided I would look into seeing if it would be possible for him to guest host on this show too—he was a natural.

The odd one out of the group was Kyun. I doubted any of the viewers would be able to pick up on it, especially as Tae and Dante were taking the lead with the answers, now that Nate was sat with the hosts. He was being very quiet—there was definitely something bothering him—but he was still able to keep his attention on who was speaking, and answer when he was asked a question directly.

And then things started to go wrong.

The next segment of the show was where the guests were given a small box, filled with questions. The only difference was they were to read the question out and direct it to one of the members themselves. The slips of paper all had the question in English and Korean, and like with the rest of the show, if they weren't confident in their question, the host would help.

For some reason, the question Kyun had only seemed to have the question in English. He scanned it a few times before taking a deep breath to attempt to read it. "When you are abroad," he read slowly, "Do you prefer to eat with chopsticks or a knife and fuck?"

I blinked, praying that I had misheard him. Judging from the murmurs in the audience, I wasn't the only one.

Nate and Bella shared a look before Bella quickly translated the question into Korean. Kyun looked confused at their reaction but nodded, and then pointed at Jun to answer the question.

I chewed at my lip. There was no way the question would have said *fuck*, and I knew Kyun wouldn't have said it intentionally, it was just how it had sounded with his accent. The letter *r* was difficult to say for non-native English speakers. But he had just cursed live on a television show which was broadcast to the world, with the two primary audiences not being broadcast after a watershed.

While Jun was busy describing how he preferred to eat pizza and that should only ever be eaten with fingers, I could see Kyun lean over to whisper in Minhyuk's ear. Seeing Minhyuk's discomfort, I assumed Kyun was asking what was up with the reaction Nate, Bella and Simon, the third host, had given his question. Minhyuk whispered something back, with a gentle, dismissive wave of his hand.

Thankfully, Jun spent a very long time talking

about pizza, and Nate shared the piece of information about Hawaiian pizza not being Hawaiian, that it was then time for the last segment: the performance of the title track.

H3RO got into place and the music started and I knew it wasn't going to go right for Kyun from the opening bars. He was half a beat behind most of the time, and on the second chorus, went into the moves of the bridge. He recovered and continued going, with a little help from Dante, but I could see he was mortified.

The end of the show couldn't come quick enough, and Kyun all but ran from the stage at the earliest opportunity. I made to go after him, but Tae grabbed my wrist. "Let me," he instructed me. I nodded and watched him go.

Nate joined my side. "It sounded like *fuck*, right?" I nodded.

"Fuck," he muttered.

"How much damage control do I need to do?" I asked. "I mean, it's obvious he was saying fork. The question was literally about cutlery—and who the hell asks that kind of question?"

"Makes a change about being asked who takes the longest in the shower," Minhyuk said, joining my side. "I could get a t-shirt printed which says *Dante would live in front of a mirror if he could* and we would still get asked that."

"Just because I look after my appearance doesn't mean I spend the longest in the bathroom," Dante objected.

He was greeted with six looks of disbelief. "Dante, I worked that out on day one," I pointed out.

"Then maybe we should get a second bathroom,"

he shrugged.

"In answer to your question," Nate interjected, folding his arms. "We can let it blow over. Kyun might become a meme for a while, but the fans will be forgiving. He has an accent: he's not American."

"But?"

"Kyun's not going to let this one go," Minhyuk sighed, sadly.

Dante nodded. "He missed a step on 'Who Is Your Hero?'."

"Shit," Nate muttered. "He's really not going to forgive himself for this one."

I was already beginning to suspect that would be the case, but I didn't like to hear it being confirmed by the others.

"If Tae's with him, he'll be OK," Jun said, joining us. "It also means we should probably avoid the green room though."

I nodded. "I think it might be for the best if you guys take one of the minibuses back first. I'll wait for Tae and Kyun. We can go separately. At least then you guys can go get some rest before we have to head back out for the next show." I went with them to the door and followed them outside to explain to security what was happening.

There was a large crowd gathered now. Not as big as the previous day's, but a size which had me grateful and not worried. Dante, Nate and Jun went straight to the barriers, trying to say hello to as many fans as possible. I glanced over at Minhyuk. "Everything OK?"

"I'm going to go back with Tae and Kyun," he told me, quietly. "If we all leave, they—Kyun—is going to think we're running out of here in embarrassment and he will be more upset."

"That's not the case though," I said, frowning.

Minhyuk shrugged. "Kyun takes it all personally. He's his own worst critic."

"OK," I agreed. Minhyuk went to join the other three in greeting the fans, while I gave the updated plans to the security detail.

I didn't rush them as we still had time, and they were happy talking to as many fans as they could, but eventually, I made Nate, Dante and Jun get in the minibus. Minhyuk followed me back inside as we went to find Tae and Kyun.

The pair were in the green room. Kyun was staring sullenly out of the window, while Tae was leaning against it, next to him, talking to him. "Hey, guys!" I called over, cheerfully. "We need to get going before they kick us out," I told them as they looked over at me.

Kyun let out an irritated grunt before he walked past me, out of the room. Tae made to follow him, but I stepped in front of him, stopping him. I waited until Minhyuk had followed after Kyun, then looked up at H3RO's leader. "Do I need to be worried?"

Tae shook his head.

"Tae," I pressed. "Do I need to be worried?"

"If you need to be worried, I'll tell you," he said, side stepping me.

I let out a long breath, bowing my head. He didn't trust me. Despite what he'd said previously, withholding who I was had definitely had an impact on our relationship.

I gave the room a once over to make sure we hadn't left anything, and then hurried after the others.

They were already outside talking to the fans by the time I arrived. I waited patiently, lurking behind them.

We slowly made our way down the fan-lined path until we arrived at the minibus. I opened up the door and Kyun went in first, waving behind him as he did. As Minhyuk went in, he too turned to wave, but he wobbled. My hand shot up instinctively, settling on the small of his back.

"GET YOUR HANDS OFF MINHYUK!" someone in the crowd screeched.

Something exploded behind me and I shoved Minhyuk into the van, as seconds later, I realized it was an egg. My eyes shot around to the fans, trying to see where it had come from, but the crowd was descending into chaos.

Out of the corner of my eye, I saw something else hurtling towards my head, but before I could react, I was being tackled to the ground. I braced myself as I fell to the ground, just as Tae let out a cry of pain. As the egg exploded above us, I thought he had been hit by it, but as the stinky gloop dripped down on me, I realized Tae was under me. "What happened? Are you alright?" I asked him. I was conscious that there was someone throwing things at us, and a whole crowd of people with phones and cameras taking photos, but my hands traveled over Tae, trying to find the source of what was causing his face to screw up in agony.

Then the security had his hands around me, pulling me to the side and grabbing Tae and bustling him into the back of the van. I struggled to my feet, grabbing my bag, and accepting Minhyuk's hand to help me in the minibus. The door was barely closed before the driver was driving off.

I scrambled over to Tae. "What's wrong? What's happened?" I asked, doing my best not to let myself go flying into Tae as we rounded a corner much faster than I would have liked. He was clutching at something, doubled over in pain. As we hit a pothole and the minibus lurched to the side, causing Tae to cry out, I focused my attention on the driver. "Unless we are being chased, can you please slow down and drive carefully before you kill anyone!" I snapped at him. "You got us out of there. Let's stay safe, OK?"

The driver nodded and slowed down. "Sorry," I heard him say.

I quickly looked at Minhyuk and Kyun. They both wore expressions I'd seen before: terror. "We're OK, guys," I assured them. Or at least some of us were. I turned back to Tae, and now the minibus was moving in a much more controlled manner, tried to get him to look at me. "Tae, what's wrong?"

"I think my arm is broken," he murmured, weakly.

"Let me see," I said, gently.

He moved back, but kept his arm still on his lap, the other hand clutching at the arm just below his elbow. In the gap between that and his wrist, was a very red, almost black, mark, about the size of a fist. Although there was no actual blood, I could see a sharp bump where the bone was close to piercing the skin.

I turned to the driver again. "Without breaking any laws, please can you take us to the nearest hospital."

"How bad is it?" Minhyuk asked, paling.

"Just a broken bone," I said, trying to come across as unconcerned. What the hell did I know? I didn't have a medical degree. It looked broken. It looked broken enough he would need a cast on it. After that, I didn't know.

What I did know was that there was no reason to panic anyone.

제11장

H3RO

Going Crazy

I cancelled our appearance on the evening show. Tae had, as he had suspected, broken his arm, and although he was whisked away to a private room, it was a while before the doctor came out. At that point, Dante, Nate and Jun had arrived at the hospital too.

"It's going to need pinning in place," the doctor explained. "And then a cast."

"What does that mean?" Tae asked. He was in bed, hooked up to an IV which was delivering him liquids and pain relief. A fair bit of pain relief considering how out of it he seemed.

"We will need to operate," the doctor told him. "I will then want you to rest for a couple of days."

"We have shows and appearances," Tae said, shaking his head. "Just put it in a cast. It doesn't hurt that much."

The doctor shook his head. "You don't hurt because the morphine we're giving you is masking that. As for your appearances, you won't be taking part in those for at least a week. After that, it will depend on what your performances are: if you had broken your leg,

I wouldn't have you dancing for at least six weeks."

"It's my job!" Tae objected.

"You haven't broken your leg," I said, holding my hands up to try to keep the peace. "But if the doctor says you aren't performing for a week, then you're not performing for a week," I said, firmly. "Tae, you're an idol. Your body is what makes you money."

"Way to make him sound like a hooker," Jun sniggered.

I shot Jun a glare as Dante clipped the back of the maknae's head, then turned back to Tae. "You sing. You dance. You need your body in working order. Right now, it's broken—literally. So, relax. After that, if we have to modify performances or just have you singing, then we will work that out later. The doctor has just said that you need an operation first anyway." I looked over at the doctor. "When will that be?"

"I'm not concerned about the break, but I am concerned about the surrounding area. I would like to wait until tomorrow afternoon to do the surgery." The doctor looked around the room and then sighed. "I appreciate that you are worried about your hyung, but it's time for you to leave. Those pain meds will kick in soon and Park Hyuntae will be asleep shortly. Also, there is a small crowd beginning to form outside and I would prefer it if you could leave before it gets unmanageable. We are a hospital, not a concert venue."

Well, this doctor didn't care for idols. But he had a point. "We should leave. I will be back tomorrow, Tae," I told him. I wasn't sure he was really listening, staring off into space. The doctor was probably right that he would be asleep soon.

We used the back entrance, and all piled into a

single minibus which took us back to the dorms. While the guys went inside, I carried on, up to the roof. Exhausted as I was, I had work to do. My phone, although on silent, hadn't stopped ringing.

It also, annoyingly, had a massive crack from where it had hit the ground in my bag. Thankfully, my iPad had survived unscathed. I called Lee Woojin and updated him on Tae's situation. Then I called Lee Sejin who proceeded to shout at me for being irresponsible for a full twenty minutes before abruptly hanging up on me. I followed that call up with one to the Atlantis PR team, so they could issue a statement on my behalf, and hopefully get my own phone to stop bleeping in my ear with other calls that were trying to connect.

In the end, I turned it off.

Then I turned it back on. Someone needed to call his parents and let them know what had happened, hopefully before they found out on the news. I hung my head, disappointed in myself. I should have made that call before Lee Woojin!

I was exceptionally grateful to learn that they hadn't found out from the television. They said they were going to pack some things and then head over. Tae came from Incheon, so it wasn't far for them.

Then I turned my phone off.

I reached for the iPad to check the news sites. If they were calling, they knew something. It also meant that the statement hadn't been released. It went up as I was scrolling.

But then other things caught my attention.

Kyun was trending.

At first, I stared at his name in confusion, and then it dawned on me. *Fuck.* Literally, fuck. I started clicking to find mixed comments. The most understanding came from the international sites, who, as I had said to the others, pointed out it was just his accent and it wasn't his intention to swear on live television. The domestic sites were less sympathetic.

That didn't bother me too much. They weren't written in the most flattering way, but they had mentioned that it was only really a mispronunciation … but the comments were brutal.

Once again, Ha Kyungu proves he shouldn't speak other languages!

Who taught him English? They need sacking!

How dare he swear on air—he brings shame on Korea!

He's an idiot!

And then they turned to comments on the overall show performance.

Who let him in H3RO? He just makes them look bad.

Bringing down the performance, the visuals and the vocals. Sack him.

Petition to remove Kyun from H3RO!

Fat pig needs to lose more weight. Then maybe he will keep up when he's dancing—oink oink!

I stared, mouth open as the comments got ruder and filled with more profanity (talk about hypocrisy). Then my rage set in. I *only* just managed to refrain from responding back to some of these comments. The last thing they needed was H3RO's manager all over this. Instead, I took screenshots of everything and sent it to the security team. They were going to be busy later.

I stretched out, working out a kink in my neck. I was livid and there was nothing immediate I could do about it.

I was also concerned about Kyun, and although he would probably hate it, I wanted to wrap him up in a blanket and cuddle him.

Thankfully, they still didn't have their own phones. If Jun still had hold of the team's iPad, hopefully Kyun wouldn't have had the opportunity to see any of the comments.

Seriously, how could people be so hateful?

And what did his appearance have to do with anything? His appearance, was, for the record hot as hell, not pig-like, or even close to being overweight. Were these people deaf? He could sing!

I set my iPad back down, feeling my anger build again. Anyone could be brave when they were hidden behind a computer screen. *Keyboard warriors.*

Gathering my things up and sliding them into my purse, I made my way to the dorm. It had gotten late, and as there was an early call in the morning, the lights were already off inside.

I flicked on the lights to the kitchen / living area, trying to see if I could spot the team's iPad. I wasn't sure if wrapping Kyun up in bubble wrap was the best thing to do, but *I* was hurt by those hateful comments and they weren't directed at me.

I groaned, resting my hands against the small kitchen island and bowing my head. I couldn't find the iPad anywhere. "Please let it be with Jun," I muttered at the worktop.

"You're bleeding."

The sound of Minhyuk's voice made me jump

and although I refrained from squealing, I did mutter a few curses under my breath.

"I'm sorry," he said, padding over to me in slippers. "I didn't mean to startle you."

"Did I wake you?" I asked, quietly, conscious that everyone else was asleep.

Minhyuk shook his head. "I couldn't sleep. But you're bleeding," he repeated. I glanced down at where he was pointing: my knees. I leaned down and prodded at it, gingerly, wincing when it hurt. Minhyuk grabbed at my hand, pulling it away. "Don't hurt yourself," he chided me gently. Still holding my hand, he led me over to the couch.

"It's not bleeding anymore," I told him. "It's starting to scab."

"It still needs cleaning, otherwise it will become infected," he said. He released me to disappear back down the hallway to the bathroom, where the first aid kit lived.

While he was gone, I pulled my skirt up to examine my legs, spotting a few scuffs and grazes. How my body hadn't reacted to them until now was a mystery, but now that I was looking at them, each one decided to start stinging.

Minhyuk reappeared as I was prodding at them again. He scowled, batting my hand away. "I bet they're not even clean!" he exclaimed, though he kept his volume down.

Silently, I shook my head. "They didn't start hurting until you pointed them out," I sulked.

He set the first aid kit down, then went to the kitchen sink to wash his hands, before waving them around in the air so they could dry. He returned to me and frowned. Carefully, Minhyuk sat beside me on the couch, and then leaned forward, scooping my legs up so they came to a rest on his thighs. He bowed his head, peering at the fresh scab on my knee. "It looks like it hurts."

I shifted my position, then leaned back against the arm of the couch. I wasn't great when it came to my own blood. I stared up at the ceiling. I could hear Minhyuk searching through the first aid kit. This was going to sting. "Tae shouldn't have done what he did," I said, quietly.

"He saved you," Minhyuk said, sounding surprised.

I raised my head to look at him. "Saving me is a bit melodramatic, Minhyuk. It was an egg. He broke his arm stopping me from getting hit by an egg. He should have just let me get hit."

"If he hadn't have done it, I would have," Minhyuk told me. "I couldn't get out of the bus fast enough."

I shook my head. "It was an egg. I've been hit by two of them already. Yes, it hurt, but I can promise you they hurt less than a broken arm."

"No one should be throwing an egg at you to start with," he said, softly.

"I completely agree with you on that point," I said with a nod of my head. "But if this happens again, please don't do anything that could risk you getting hurt like that. I'm not sure I could cope with it." I sank back down and stared up at the ceiling again.

If I could sum up how I felt these days, using only one word, it would be 'guilty'. I had been hiding who I was. I still hadn't decided what I was doing with the two-thirds of H3RO I was kissing, and now Tae was lying in a hospital bed because some crazy fan had decided I was fooling around with him. The irony was she wasn't wrong and I kind of deserved it. But Tae didn't.

"I'm sorry," Minhyuk said, softly.

"This is going to hurt, isn't it?" I sighed, screwing up my face as I tried to prepare for the pain that would come as he cleaned the wounds with antiseptic liquid.

"No, I mean for this."

I relaxed my face as I pulled myself up to look at him again. He was staring down at my knee, but his hands were empty of anything. "It's OK," I said. "I won't pretend I'm going to like it, but you're right: they need cleaning before they get infected."

Minhyuk slowly shook his head. "No, I mean for *all* of this. I'm the reason you got hurt."

I pulled a face. "You?"

He nodded. "Yeah."

"Technically, it was Tae who pulled me down, but if we're going to lay the blame on anyone, it can go on the psycho who thinks it's fun to throw things at people," I corrected him. "It's not your fault, nor is it Tae's."

Minhyuk turned to face me then, and he looked miserable. His usual cheerful expression was missing, replaced with lips that turned down in the corners and eyes, almost hidden behind his hair, that looked as guilty as I was feeling these days. "It is my fault."

I pushed myself upright, bringing me close to him. Resting my forearms on my thighs, I peered at him with a frown. "How is it your fault?"

"She shouted at you because of me," he

mumbled, although he didn't look away.

I frowned, trying to work out what he was talking about, then it dawned on me. "She told me to take my hands off you. My hand was on you, not the other way around," I pointed out. "That puts me in the wrong, not you."

Minhyuk dropped his head. "But I don't mind you touching me," he muttered.

"That's good," I agreed, lightheartedly. "Otherwise this situation would be a lot more awkward than it needed to be."

"She acted that way because of me," he said, turning back to me.

I shrugged. "I don't care if she likes you, or if she likes H3RO as a whole. She is responsible for her own actions. Unless of course, you know who she is, and you asked her to do that," I added with a smile, trying to lighten the mood.

Instead, Minhyuk looked mortified as his eyes widened at me. "I would *never* do that. I like you!"

"Don't worry," I said with a light giggle, leaning over to place a hand on his leg. "I was joking. I know you wouldn't do anything like that."

Minhyuk's attention fell to my hand. "You don't understand," he sighed.

I gave him another smile, accompanied by a reassuring squeeze. "I do, and it's not what you think, Minhyuk. I don't blame any of this on you, or any of H3RO, to be clear. There's just one fan out there who's doing this for whatever reason she has in her head." Hopefully it was just one fan, after all, it was eggs being thrown all the time … "Maybe I need to start wearing a jacket with 'manager' on the back?" I added as an afterthought. Actually, that didn't seem like such a bad idea.

"You still don't understand," he said. His hand reached for mine as he looked nervously at me.

"OK," I said slowly. Minhyuk was usually cheerful: the others had frequently dubbed him the mood-maker of H3RO. He was certainly the first one to smile, as well as the first one to struggle to keep that smile from his face at a photoshoot. I wasn't used to him being this serious and upset. That worried me more than I would have thought. "Explain to me what you mean," I offered gently. Maybe that way I could explain it to him as to why none of this was his fault with his own words.

"I like you," he said again.

I nodded. "I know, but that doesn't make it OK for anyone to throw things at people."

"No!" Minhyuk snapped. "You're not listening to me. I think you are smart, and pretty, and confident. I love how you look in dresses and how you wear them all the time. I love how you always ask me what I'm cooking, offer to help, and then listen to me when I tell you my little cooking tricks. You always take the time after a show to tell me I did well, even when we both know I got something wrong. You're sweet and kind, and I like you!"

I blinked, trying to process the words I was hearing, mentally translating them to English, as though that would clarify what I was hearing.

Then Minhyuk shocked me even further. He leaned over and kissed me.

제12 장

H3R오

Calling You

I froze, too in shock to respond, and then Minhyuk pulled away looking mortified. "I'm sorry," he said. He let go of my hand and started to wiggle out from under me.

"Wait," I said, grabbing his hand. "I … just … don't go," I told him.

He shook his head, still trying to make his getaway. "No, I'm sorry, I shouldn't have done that."

"Just wait," I said, pulling him back down with a little more force than was necessary, but I didn't want him leaving like this. Not while I was still trying to get my brain to actually make words string together into coherent sentences.

Minhyuk sat down but refused to look at me. On the plus side, he didn't pull his hand free from mine.

"I like you too," I admitted—apparently to myself as well as to him. "I like you," I said, saying the words again. They didn't feel wrong … oh holy hell, I was in trouble. I raked my free hand through my hair. "I like you too," I sighed.

Minhyuk slowly turned to me, his eyes full of

hope. "You do?" he asked, hesitantly.

I nodded, chewing my lip. "But it's not as simple as that," I said slowly. "I'm your manager. And the others …" I trailed off, not sure how I could even begin to explain that.

"So long as I like you, which I do, and you like me …?" he looked at me questioningly. I sighed but nodded. "Which you do, we can work the rest of it out."

"Minhyuk," I said, softly. "It's more complicated than that. You don't understand."

"No. What's *simpler* than two people who like each other?" he asked. With his free hand, he reached over and cupped my face. "It becomes complicated when we allow it to."

Unfortunately, I had already made it complicated. He just didn't know that part yet.

He leaned in towards me. Although his hand was still on my cheek, it wasn't restrictive, meaning I had the ability to move if I wanted to.

I didn't.

I didn't know what I wanted.

I did know I wanted to kiss him.

But I also didn't want to hurt him too. "Minhyuk," I said, his name in a barely audible whisper.

I'd wanted it to stop him, but saying his name had the opposite effect. His lips met mine, gently. Pausing there, just long enough for my own to get accustomed to their softness. I'd never seen him with chap stick, unless it was being applied for him, but he had the softest lips I'd kissed. I had only just realized that when he pulled away.

My hand tightened around his, and before he could get too far, I leaned into him, tilting my head.

Minhyuk's movements were gentle, reserved almost. For a moment, I wasn't sure if he was regretting his decision, and then I realized that wasn't the case. The bubbliest member of H3RO, the one with his own hoard of fangirls, was unsure.

While making sure not to break the kiss, I shuffled closer to him, trying to make the angle between us a little less awkward. Comfortable, I started to pull at his lower lip, teasing it with my tongue. When he got the hint, parting his lips, I swept my tongue inside, taking the lead. He didn't seem to mind. If anything, he seemed to relax more, his hand joining the other on my face, gripping at me like I was providing him with oxygen, not kisses.

Again, and again, our tongues and lips met, as he grew in confidence. I was being selfish now, and I knew it. Someone was going to get hurt here, and it shouldn't be Minhyuk.

I pulled away, my swollen lips already missing his, and found him breathing heavily, a hazy look settling over him. "Minhyuk," I sighed, his name already sounding like an apology.

"Don't," he muttered. "Don't ruin this."

A knot formed in my stomach. No, it was already there. The knot grew and tightened. I was going to hell and I deserved nothing less.

Minhyuk gave me a shy smile, then moved further down the couch, picking up the previously discarded antibacterial wipes. Still smiling to himself, he leaned over and started cleaning my wounds.

Even though it hurt, I didn't allow myself to wince once.

H3RⓄ

By morning, I swear that knot in my stomach had grown again. I had no appetite, especially when Minhyuk leaned over to add some beansprouts to my rice. "You OK?" Jun asked me.

I glanced up and found him watching me. Did he know? He seemed to know about everyone else. He was looking at me with concern though. Maybe not? My stomach churned and I pushed the bowl away, trying to find something else to focus on. "Where's Kyun?" I asked, suddenly realizing there was a face missing at the table.

"Still in bed?" Jun offered.

I got to my feet, thankful for an excuse to leave the table, and all but ran to the room Kyun shared with Tae. I tapped on the door. When I didn't get a response, I frowned. Kyun was usually an early riser.

I knocked again, louder this time. "Kyun-*ah*?" I called, gently. When I still had no response, I pushed the door open. "Kyun?" I frowned. "I'm going to turn the light on," I warned him. With no response, I did just that.

Their room wasn't that big. Given the overall size of the dorm they shared, this was of no surprise. None of the rooms were particularly big. Jun and Nate had a room so small it could only fit a bunkbed in. At least they had a bed—Dante and Minhyuk had roll down bedding. They assured me they were used to it. Personally, I would have been lost without the three-quarter mattress I had.

As leader, Tae had a bed, and by default, so did Kyun. Their room was big enough to walk around the two single beds, though, at some point since they started sharing, they had pushed them together. At this present moment in time, both halves of the bed were empty and didn't even looked slept in.

The knot of guilt in my stomach was replaced with worry. This didn't feel right. I stepped out, walking straight into Jun. His hand grabbed my arm to steady me. "Are you OK?"

I shook my head. "Where is Kyun?"

Jun peered around me with a frown, then he walked down the short hallway to the bathroom, pushing the door open. He looked back to me and shook his head. "Empty."

I hurried back to the living room. "Has anyone seen Kyun? He's not in his room."

"He could be in the gym?" Minhyuk suggested.

"Do you want me to go check?" Jun offered, already halfway to the door.

"No," I said, calling him back. "You guys need to be in a minibus in fifteen minutes. Gather your stuff together and meet me downstairs. I'll go and check the basement."

The building with the dorms had two private gyms in the basement. Since moving in, I had learned that the lower levels of the building were occupied only by the males (well, aside from me, but H3RO seemed to be the only ones aware of that), and the upper levels were occupied by the females. The basement had been split into two gyms—one for each sex.

As there were many trainees, rookies and experienced idols sharing the dorm, the gyms usually had a few people in it, even at this time of morning. I walked in, nearly knocking two guys down. It was the

Chinese members of Onyx and B.W.B.B., Xiao and Sun.

I stared at them, my mind going temporarily blank at the sight of two chiseled, bare, sweaty chests. *Holy hell*, Atlantis Entertainment had some smoking hot guys signed to them.

"Is everything OK, Miss Holly?" Xiao asked.

"This is the men's gym," Sun added, using his head to nod in the direction of the gym behind him.

I nodded, trying not to come across as worried as I felt. "Can one of you head in there and grab Kyun for me? We've got an appearance to get to."

Xiao and Sun shared a look. "Kyun's not in here," Xiao told me, carefully.

"Are you sure?" I asked with a frown.

Xiao stepped back into the room, staring down the far end of it. "King," he yelled, making me jump.

A younger male wearing only a towel stepped out of a doorway. Lee Minhyuk, aka King, (not related to me, and one of the many Minhyuks who seemed to be on the Atlantis roster), was one of the solo artists signed to the label and the same age as my younger half-brother, Seungjin. As soon as he saw me, his eyes went wide, dropping to his towel, then, even though it was firmly in place, he clutched at it, jumping back behind the door so only his head was visible. "*Hyung!*"

"That's cruel," I muttered at Xiao, though my lips were twitching to smile.

Xiao gave me a sly look as he grinned. "Funny though." He turned back to the younger male. "Is Kyun in there?"

King frowned, disappearing into the room. He quickly reappeared and shook his head. "Just me, hyung."

"Sorry, Miss Holly," Xiao apologized, turning back to me.

"Thank you," I muttered, turning and leaving them to it. I made my way to the minibus. The other members of H3RO were already waiting for me, and their expressions turned to ones of worry as I drew close, without Kyun.

"He wasn't there?" Dante asked.

"Obviously," Jun muttered, earning himself a clip to the ear.

"Could he have gone to see Tae?" Nate offered. "I can't remember the last time those two didn't share a room."

"That's a good call," Minhyuk said, nodding his head. "If Tae has surgery today, I bet he'd want to see him before that."

I sighed. I didn't quite understand the relationship Tae and Kyun had, but I had hoped that Kyun would have at least left a note. I had been warned before I started managing H3RO that Kyun had terrible timekeeping and would frequently miss shows due to ill health, but this wasn't bad timekeeping, nor was it *his* ill health.

I rubbed at my forehead, and then I sighed again. "OK, you guys get to the studio. If we can at least have you with your hair and makeup done, we might be able to salvage this." I frowned. *Now* was an occasion where it would have been useful if they had a phone each.

"Would you like company?" Minhyuk offered.

"You guys need to get to the studio," I repeated, even though I would have liked company. "We're already a member down." I frowned again. "Who normally steps up when Tae's out?"

The five members shared a look. "We've never been without Tae," Nate responded for them.

"OK," I said with a shrug. "Who wants to step up and be leader?"

Jun's hand shot up. That of course earned him a jab in the side. "We're not having our maknae as a leader," Dante told him, rolling his eyes.

Fair point.

"Dante?"

Dante shook his head. "I'm Chinese."

I looked at Nate, who also shook his head. "American."

When Minhyuk held his hands up and said 'maknae line', I folded my arms in frustration. "Guys, we don't have time for this. Please."

"I'll do it," said Nate.

"Thank you," I said, turning to the two members of security who were waiting patiently for us. "These guys are going to the studio. I need to get to the hospital."

We said our goodbyes and went to our respective minibus. The security guy with me was not the chatty kind, for which I was grateful. I had a bad feeling that I couldn't shake.

Of course, it wasn't visiting hours when I arrived. I had to kick up a fuss, threatening with lawyers and everything I had at my disposal to get in with Tae. I hated doing it, but I did it anyway. When I went into Tae's room, he was awake, but alone.

"Holly?" he said in surprise. "What are you doing here?"

"Where is he, Tae?" I asked as I stuck my head

into the bathroom. Kyun wasn't there.

"Who?" Tae asked, carefully.

I turned back to Tae, the panic rising. This wasn't about missing a show now. "Kyun. Where is Kyun. He's gone missing."

"What do you mean he's gone missing?"

"I mean just that!" I all but shrieked at him as I started pacing back and forth. "I can't find Kyun anywhere. We're due at a show, and he's nowhere to be found, and I couldn't give a flying monkey about this show anymore, but I can't find him."

"Hey!" he called, gently. "Come here."

"I don't need to go there, I need to find Kyun." I was verging on something between anger and hysterics, and I did my best to calm myself down. This wasn't Tae's fault.

"Don't make me get my injured body out of the bed, Holly, because it hurts," Tae warned me.

I stared at him, the guilt trip working, and hurried over. With his good hand, he reached out and took mine. "Just breathe," he muttered.

I closed my eyes and took a few deep breaths, fighting back the building anxiety. No matter what I thought had happened to Kyun, or what had actually happened to Kyun, panicking would only get me in a state and it wouldn't help anyone. "Kyun went back to the apartment with us after we left you here last night. He wasn't in his room this morning. I don't think he slept in the bed," I told him.

I opened my eyes and found Tae watching me. "He was upset after yesterday's show," he said slowly. "But he doesn't normally do things like this. Not without telling me."

"Only you're here, Tae," I said, my heart speeding up again. "I know he doesn't trust me, but I would have thought he would trust one of the others." With a hand balled up into a fist, I rubbed at my chest bone. "I should have checked on him. I should have checked if he had seen any of the comments—"

Tae's grip on my other hand tightened. "What comments?"

I reached into my bag and pulled out my phone, opening it to the photo album and the screen shots I'd taken the night before, offering it to Tae. He took it and skipped through them, his eyes scanning each comment. "Damnit!" he exclaimed under his breath. He dropped the phone and then ran a hand through his tousled hair. "Damnit!" he exclaimed again, louder this time.

He started to pull back the covers. I gaped at him in horror, reaching over to push him back down. "Tae! You're having surgery in a couple of hours! That break isn't even in a cast!"

As he moved his broken arm at the same time, he let out a cry of pain, then sat back, throwing himself against his fluffed up pillows in defeat. "Damnit!"

"What's wrong, Tae? What don't I know?" I demanded, the panic returning. "Is Kyun in trouble?"

"No," Tae snapped. Then he shook his head, screwing up his face. "I don't think so."

"Tae!" I cried.

"OK," he said, shaking his head. "I'm going to tell you something. Something that even the others don't know, OK? This is Kyun's secret."

제13 장

H3R오

Runaway

"I've known Kyun since middle school. Even though he's a couple of years younger, everyone knew who he was. He had no friends. He was always wearing tatty, ill-fitting clothes, and no one would go near him because of how bad he smelled. One day I caught him going through the school trash cans to find food."

I sank into the chair next to the bed, staring up at Tae in shock.

"I took him home with me that day. My mom didn't ask any questions. We gave him some of my old clothes, made him take a very long bath, and fed him until he couldn't eat anymore. That night, he stayed with us. Then the next night, then the next. Four *weeks* later, he went home."

"What happened?" I asked.

Tae slowly shook his head. "There's only so much of Kyun's secret I will tell you. The rest is up to him."

"That's fair," I agreed. I didn't think I would like to hear that story, and I certainly wasn't sure I was ready to hear it now.

"By high school, he was living with me. After going so long without regular meals, he would eat as much as he could and put on weight. Then H3RO happened. I'm the reason he's doing this," he sighed. "Don't get me wrong, Kyun is a great singer, and he loves what he's doing, but I know it's hard for him. He got so used to sleeping with me that he didn't think he could not do it, so he auditioned too. He was that good, he was selected before me."

I chewed at my lip, trying to work out what he was telling me. In the end, I shook my head at him. "I don't understand," I admitted.

"No, I don't think I'm explaining this well," Tae agreed. "It's hard when I can't tell you everything, and I promise you, it's not because I don't trust you. I'm telling you because I do." He scratched at the back of his head. "Kyun is my little brother. I don't just mean in H3RO, but in life. He is the guy I trust more than anyone else in the world. He didn't have an easy time growing up, and he struggles with his self-confidence. It is always the same when it comes to comeback time. He puts pressure on himself to lose weight because he doesn't think he looks good enough, and because Lee Sejin is always telling him he's fat."

"I wish he could see himself the way I did," I said. I felt like I was going to cry.

"As do I," Tae muttered in agreement. "It was manageable until about three years ago. We did a show where we were asked to speak in English. Like he did the other day, he got a word wrong. Then SNS went crazy, and three years ago it wasn't nearly as bad as it is now."

"That's why he always looks so panicked when I

mention speaking English," I realized. "Oh, god, I wish I'd known."

"About that time, he ended up with an anti-fan."

"A what now?" I asked, alarmed.

"Exactly what it sounds like," Tae murmured. "The opposite of a fan. They don't support us. They hate us. They try to do all that they can to bring us down."

"And H3RO has one?" My mouth fell open as I reached for my phone.

Tae grabbed my hand before I could get to my phone. "We probably do, but this one is Kyun's. She hates him."

"Who is she?" I demanded.

"This was three years ago," Tae said, trying to pacify me.

It didn't work. "I don't care if it was the day after you debuted."

"Holly," he sighed. "I don't like her, but this isn't her. I'm trying to explain to you where Kyun is."

I pulled my hand free and started pacing back and forth. I was still so angry I was shaking, and this was the only thing I could think of to try to calm me down. "Is she one of the people who commented?"

Tae shook his head. "I didn't recognize any of the usernames. The thing is though, she picked up on his weakness: his self-confidence. None of us want to mess up, but the rest of us are better at picking ourselves up, or, laughing it off. Not Kyun."

"He didn't say the wrong word though!" I exclaimed. "It was obvious to everyone he just mispronounced fork."

"It's not the English that will be upsetting him the

most," Tae told me.

"Then what?" I demanded. Then it hit me. "His dancing."

"He has been getting better over the last few years, possibly because we've not been in the spotlight, but I can usually pull him out of his self-confidence dips. It's when he does something which he thinks affects us negatively. If he messes up a dance move, he makes H3RO look bad. And he's definitely heard it enough from management to believe it."

I stopped pacing, wondering how much of this was self-inflicted, and how much of it originated from Lee Sejin. By all accounts, while H3RO gave him an escape it also gave him another form of imprisonment. "Where can I find him, Tae?" I asked, gently.

"I told you this because I trust you," Tae said again. I nodded. "You need to know, to understand, but you can't let Kyun know that you know."

"Tae," I stopped, the words getting stuck in my throat. "Tae, where is he?"

"He can't know," he emphasized.

"I won't tell him anything," I promised. "Please."

"He's probably in our old practice studio," Tae finally told me. "Before the basement was converted into the gyms, they had our studios. The dorms got refurbished just after Onyx debuted. They put gyms below and the studios got moved to the Atlantis building. Except for one. It had the building's boiler in it, so they kept the studio as it was and built the gyms around it."

"Thank you," I said, relieved. "I'm going there now. I'll be back later."

"I'm trusting you, Holly," he called after me.

I was still shaking when I got outside to where the minibus was waiting for me. I instructed the driver to take me back to the dorms, praying that Kyun was there. At this point, we had to contend with rush hour traffic.

By the time we arrived at the dorms, I was sure I was about to have a meltdown. Instead of waiting for the elevator, I charged down the stairs, seeking out the room Tae had been talking about. I ran past the two gyms, then came to the last room down there—I'd never seen it before as I'd never needed to go further than the female gym I'd barely used.

I paused outside, trying to get my breathing under control. If Tae was right and Kyun was in here, I didn't want him to be alarmed at my sudden appearance.

I sucked in one last breath, smoothed my hair down for good measure, and then pushed the door open. I could hear 'Who Is Your Hero?' as soon as I pushed open the door. I could also hear movement. Both of which sent such a strong feeling of relief rushing over me, I could have cried.

Instead, I stepped into the room. I wasn't sure how big this room had been before the refurb had taken place, but it looked like it had been chopped in half at least. The bottom of the room had the boiler Tae had mentioned. Although the summer months meant there was no need for heating in the building, it was still needed for the hot water. With so many people living in the high rise, I suspected it was always on. As such, the room was hot and stuffy.

One wall had a floor to ceiling mirror on it that Kyun was dancing in front of. His t-shirt was soaked in sweat. So were his jogging bottoms. There was sweat running down the side of his neck, and even his hair looked wet enough that he could have just walked out of the shower. Hell, the same could be said about everything he was wearing.

He looked completely exhausted.

Then he made me jump by swearing loudly. "No, stupid!" he yelled at his reflection, marching over to the music player.

"Here you are!" I called, brightly, before he could start the music again. "I've been looking everywhere for you."

"How did you know I was here?" he asked, looking startled at my appearance.

I walked over, trying not to wince. Up close he looked even worse. "I was checking the gym. I heard the music," I lied. What was one more lie at this point? "What are you doing down here? Aren't the studios at Atlantis better than this? Or at least air conditioned."

Kyun looked at his reflection, as though seeing himself for the first time. "Oh," he muttered. "I messed up the routine," he told me, simply.

"I didn't notice," I shrugged. "But it's only a practice. I bet you've been at this for a while now anyway."

"No," he said, shaking his head. "On the show today."

"Yesterday," I corrected him, softly. Kyun frowned at me. "It's nearly 9 a.m.," I clarified. "The show was yesterday. How long have you been here?"

"After we got back from the hospital," he muttered, looking a little dazed.

"Have you eaten?" I asked. "I know it's a bit boring, but I was going to make porridge if you want to join me?"

Kyun nodded suddenly sagging as though he realized he was exhausted. He nodded, then switched the CD player off. Together we walked out and took the elevator up to our dorm.

I pushed the door open and let him in. "Why don't you go shower while I get the porridge cooking?" Kyun nodded numbly, then disappeared down the corridor. As soon as I could hear the water running, I pulled out my phone and called the executive who had booked us on the show. I apologized profusely that Tae was in surgery, and Kyun had come down with the flu and asked if he would mind passing his phone to someone in the group.

"Have you found him?" Nate asked.

"I've got him," I confirmed, quietly, keeping an eye on the hallway. "But it's just going to be the four of you. He's not going to make it to the show."

"Is he OK?" Nate asked. I could hear the others behind him asking a dozen questions.

"He will be. Will you guys be able to cope?"

"Don't worry about us," Nate assured me. "We've got this."

"Flu," I said, quickly. "He's got the flu."

I hung up and turned my attention to the kitchen. I wasn't much of a cook, at least not when it came to Korean food, but I could make porridge. When Kyun emerged, it was ready for dishing up. "Go sit on the couch," I instructed him. He looked ready to drop. I joined him moments later, carrying two bowls of porridge.

"Thank you," he said, taking it from me. He eyed it suspiciously, but as soon as he had one mouthful, he wolfed the rest down.

I sat next to him, still eating mine, while he stared at his empty bowl. I was trying to work out how to talk to him about what was happening with him, without letting on I knew anything.

"The studios are soundproof," he said, suddenly.

My spoon had been halfway to my mouth, and it hovered there. "Huh?"

"You couldn't have heard me from the gym because the walls are soundproofed."

I set the spoon and the bowl down on the floor with a sigh. "You weren't in your bedroom and it looked like you hadn't slept in it either: I got worried," I told him. "I went looking for you."

Kyun was silent again.

"Look, you're not a prisoner here, and you don't need to tell me personally, but you've got to tell someone where you are, especially when you have a schedule."

"Schedule?" Kyun repeated, his eyes going wide with panic. "I'm supposed to be on a show now?"

I held my hands up. "It's OK, the others are there."

"I should be there," he cried, getting to his feet.

"Kyun, even if we left now, we wouldn't get there in time. Don't worry about it."

"But I'm letting them down!" he protested.

I shook my head. "No, you're not. Do I look worried?" I asked him, calmly.

He paused and looked at me. "Won't I get into trouble?"

"From who? Your manager?"

"Lee Sejin?"

I shrugged. "Guy's an asshole: I don't give a shit

what he thinks." I nodded to the space he vacated. "If you want to get more porridge while you're up, do so, otherwise sit back down."

He hesitated. "I should go back to the dance studio. If I'm not on the show, I should be practicing."

"Kyun," I sighed.

"I saw the comments," he said abruptly.

I refrained from swearing aloud. "You're not the first idol to forget their routine, and you won't be the last," I said, evenly. "And there will always be trolls who will comment on that. But they will forget about it by tomorrow."

"It doesn't mean they're not right," he said, miserably.

"Well it depends on what comments you're talking about," I told him sharply. "Because yes, you did mess up a dance routine, and yes, you did mispronounce a word, but those were mistakes and *I* know you wouldn't have done them intentionally, as does every other sane person with half a braincell." I stared up at him then decided to just say it. "As for the ones relating to your appearance? Kyun, you're one of the most handsome men I've ever laid eyes on. And I mean that—I think you are gorgeous." I could feel my neck heat up as he stared down at me with a weird intensity I'd not experienced from him before. "Just because you have a different build to the others doesn't mean there's anything wrong with you," I continued, rambling. "Which, for the record, is not me calling you fat or anything close to it! So, if you're talking about those comments, then I would completely disagree and would say that not only are they all wrong, but you are too."

I trailed off, feeling embarrassed. I meant every

word I said, but there were more eloquent ways of saying it. Plus, he'd not specifically mentioned anything about the comments on his appearance. Would he know what I was talking about? Would he now go check?

I stood up, gathering his bowl and walking over to the kitchen. I filled his bowl up and turned, ready to take it back to him, but found him right behind me. I stuck the bowl out towards him, and he took it.

"Please don't be upset about your English," I said, quietly. "It's a lot better than you think, but if you're not happy speaking it, I will make sure that in future you don't have to. I will make it an actual requirement if I have to."

"My English isn't good," he said, shaking his head at me. "I have to translate everything in my head, and then I don't get it right."

"There was a point when your Korean wasn't very good," I told him. "And I know you speak Japanese, and there will have been a time when that wasn't good too. I mean it when I say I will make sure you don't have to speak English, but if you do want to learn, I will teach you."

I moved back to the couch and settled back down, picking up my porridge. It had gone cold and I didn't have much of an appetite for it, but I continued to eat it anyway as Kyun sat down beside me.

"H3RO means everything to me," he said, staring at his bowl.

I nodded. "I know."

"I don't want to let them down."

"I don't think there's anybody who thinks you have," I assured him.

"But the articles—"

"Were they written by any of the members?" I asked. "Did any of them comment on it?" I shook my head. "We can ask them when they get back from the show if you'd like?"

"The show I was supposed to be on with them," he muttered, sounding disgusted with himself as he set the bowl on the floor.

I twisted in my seat, mainly so I could see him better. "Kyun, I say this whilst reminding you that I think you're ridiculously handsome, but you look awful right now. Your schedule is crazy, and the last couple of days where we've actually had a lull, have you had a break?" I asked him. "Or have you spent the whole time down in that dance studio?"

He finally looked at me then, so exhausted, so defeated, I thought I had broken him. "I can't sleep," he whispered. "I can't sleep at all when Tae isn't here: I can't sleep alone."

I could see the panic in his eyes, like just thinking about it was causing his anxiety to rocket. I shuffled over and wrapped an arm around his shoulder. "OK," I said gently. "Kyun, I'm worried about you. I'm going to take you to see a doctor later, and if he says we need to give you a timeout from promotions, we're going to do that."

Kyun jerked back, his eyes wide. "I can't do that! I can't let H3RO down!"

I held my hands up. "Making sure you are well is not letting H3RO down," I told him, firmly. "But if you're not sleeping and worrying that much then *I*, as your manager, am letting you down. You're more important than a few television shows."

"The fans—"

"Will understand," I cut him off. "How many times do they ask you if you're sleeping and eating, and tell you to look after yourself?" I could feel the tears pricking at the corner of my eyes, and I fought to keep them at bay. "We haven't seen the doctor yet. He might say everything is OK, but if he says that you need to take a short timeout, isn't that a good thing?"

"I'm just tired," Kyun tried again. "And I can't sleep by myself."

"Then sleep with me until Tae is released from hospital," I offered. He looked up at me and nodded. Gently, I pulled him to me, so he could lay his head down in my lap. He curled his legs up behind him. "A timeout isn't a sign of weakness, Kyunnie," I murmured as I gently ran my fingers through his hair.

Slowly, he relaxed against me, his chest rising and falling steadily. Only then did I turn my head away and let the tears silently fall.

제14 장

H3RO

While You Were Sleeping

My leg fell asleep, but I didn't move. Even in his sleep, he was frowning, but he *was* asleep. At some point, I wiped my tears away. My heart genuinely ached for him. A couple of hours later, the door opened. My finger shot to my lips with a hiss. Minhyuk, who was first through the door, stopped, saw what was happening, and stepped back, closing the door again.

There were muffled objections from outside, then it went quiet. Minhyuk opened the door again, and the four members walked in somberly, all looking over at us. Before any of them could say anything, I shook my head. "Later," I mouthed at them.

Dante looked over at the two of us, frowned, then dragged Jun off towards the bedrooms. I was thankful. Despite his best intentions, Jun was the one most likely to wake him. Minhyuk looked over at the kitchen and then set to, clearing up the porridge bowls as quietly as possible.

Nate came over and perched on the arm of the couch beside me. "Is he OK?" he asked in a low murmur.

I glanced down at Kyun. I hadn't stopped stroking his head, lazily running my fingers through his hair. "He will be," I muttered. "Did the show go OK?"

Nate nodded. "Dante and Jun took Kyun and Tae's parts. Jun sang completely the wrong lyrics."

"Is he OK?" I asked. I didn't care the lyrics were wrong, but I wasn't sure if Jun was upset about it.

"We joked about it with the MCs after," Nate shrugged. "Jun found it hilarious, as Jun would." He looked at me with a frown. "Are you OK? You look like you've been crying."

"Nothing a night of drinking and dancing wouldn't cure," I grinned, wryly. "But yes, I'm fine." I glanced at the clock. "You guys have a radio show in a couple of hours. You should have gone straight there."

"We wanted to check in with you and Kyun-*ah*," Nate told me.

"I can do it," Kyun mumbled from my lap.

"Kyun," I sighed, not wanting to make a fuss in front of Nate, but equally not wanting him to do something which was going to cause him stress.

Kyun rolled onto his back and looked up at me. For the first time in a while, he looked calm. "I will go see a doctor, but I want to continue with promotions."

I could sense Nate staring at me, his gaze boring into the side of my head, but I focused on Kyun. "OK," I agreed, gently. "But you are going to see the doctor tomorrow."

Kyun stared up at me, unblinking, and then nodded. "OK," he said, repeating my words. "I'll go see the doctor tomorrow." He then got up, stretched and headed back to his bedroom.

"Holly, what the hell?" Nate asked in surprise.

"I'm making sure he's OK," I said, wearily.

"Thank you," Nate said, so solemnly he surprised *me*. "We've all been worried, but Tae has always said he will handle it."

I nodded, then got up so I could get ready to leave. It was late afternoon, but it felt like the longest day yet.

H3RO

While H3RO were on the radio, I went to the hospital to check on Tae. He had come out of surgery and although it wasn't visiting hours, the staff must have remembered my earlier fuss because they let me in to see him straight away. "How are you doing?" I asked him.

"How's Kyun? Did you find him?"

I took one of the armchairs next to the bed. His room was filled with so many flowers and presents, it was like being in a gift shop. "He was practicing as you said," I nodded. "I took him back to the dorm, gave him something to eat and let him have a nap. He's currently on air," I said, pulling out my iPad. I loaded up the online station so we could listen to it in the background.

"Is he OK?"

"He will be," I assured Tae. "I'm taking him to a doctor tomorrow."

Tae's eyes went wide. "He won't go for that. Atlantis won't go for that."

"He's already agreed," I told him. I crossed my legs and settled into the chair. "I also don't give a shit what Lee Sejin thinks about it either. Kyun is hurting and it's our responsibility to look after him.

"I tried, you know," Tae said, hanging his head.

"I'm not a doctor, and I don't know the ins and outs of what's going on with Kyun," I sighed. "But I don't doubt for one second that the reason he's gotten as far as he has, for so long, is because he's had you. Which is also why I'm here."

"I don't understand," Tae said, slowly.

"I wanted to check up on you," I told him.

"Huh?"

I smiled sadly. "This world is crazy. You guys get so caught up going from one promotion to another, with little rest, worrying about what the world and what Atlantis, specifically my asshole half-demon relation, thinks, that I wonder if anyone has ever asked any of you if you're all OK? Add in your added responsibility as leader, looking after Kyun, and the pressure of this last comeback, I'm worried about you."

"I'm fine," Tae assured me, though he was giving me a look that I couldn't quite decide if it was suspicion, or something else.

"I just wanted you to know that I'm going to arrange for someone to be available if you're ever getting stressed out and need to talk," I said.

I stayed and listened to the show with him, leaving only when the nurses started getting annoyed by my presence. He was free to be discharged soon.

Instead of going back to the dorm, I went to Atlantis. After checking in with Park Inhye, Lee Sejin's secretary (but an actual wonderful human being), I discovered that Atlantis had someone they used for instances like this and managed to book an appointment for Kyun in the morning.

Then I made my way to my office. I wanted to check what was in the boxes before I let *any* of them into the dorms.

I spent several hours there, giving the letters little more than a skim over, before carefully retuning them to their envelopes. There were a few that genuinely made me smile with their thoughtfulness which made me give them a second look, but I wasn't interested in their content.

I was hunting out anything nasty.

And boy did I find it. Letters that went into graphic detail of what they wanted to do to various members (some at the same time), which wasn't too bad, but there was a lot which involved violence. There was one wishing for a snuff film to be made with them—they wanted to be filmed dying as Minhyuk choked the air out of them. That made me shudder. There was no way in hell I was ever letting that one get in front of Minhyuk. They went into a separate box to be dropped off at security on my way out of the building. I wasn't sure what could be done about them, but at the very least, I was making sure no one in H3RO ever got to read the vile messages.

By the time I got into the dorm, it was late. I had spent hours going through the letters, and only touched a quarter of the boxes. I had brought one of them back with me and I left it on the kitchen island for the guys to read when they had the chance.

What I'd also checked were all the private messages on the SNS.

And wow, I wished I hadn't.

Some were acceptable. Some were hilarious—sassy responses to some of the posts. But then there were the ones where some fans (of both sexes), had decided to send nudes.

And the hate messages …

I took screen shots of them all and then turned off the private messaging for everything that had it. I couldn't stop the comments on the posts, but the ones sent in private were much worse. I once again forwarded them all on to the security team.

I was exhausted and all I wanted was to sleep. I crawled into my bed and fell asleep almost instantly.

Which was why it felt odd when I woke up a short while later. Something seemed off. I turned my head, curious as to what it was, and nearly screamed at the figure standing above me. It was only because I recognized the profile in the dim light that I didn't. "Kyun!" I exclaimed in a hushed whisper. "What are you doing here?"

He hovered by my bed. "You said I could sleep with you," he said, sheepishly, hanging his head and hugging his pillow to him.

I had … I hadn't really thought he would ever take me up on that though.

Regardless, I *had* said that. I shuffled over to make room and lifted my blanket up. Awkwardly, Kyun got in beside me. We both lay there, on our backs, staring up at the ceiling.

Finally, after letting out a long and deep sigh, Kyun turned his head. "Thank you," he said, quietly.

I wasn't quite sure what he was thanking me for, but I nodded regardless. "Get some sleep, Kyun," I muttered.

H3RO

"Holly, Kyun's ... here ..."

My eyes flew open and my brain tried to work out what the hell was going on. It took a few seconds to work out Jun was in the doorway, staring down at me. Then I was aware of the body wrapped around mine. I glanced down and found Kyun, still asleep.

"This isn't what it looks like," I whispered to Jun. For once.

I almost laughed at that: this *was* completely innocent.

Jun shrugged. "Don't care if it is." Then he backed out of the room and quietly closed the door.

I lay back and closed my eyes. My life was a mess. And what the hell did that mean? *Don't care if it is*? "Life is complicated," I muttered.

Kyun snuggled deeper into my shoulder, his arms tightening their grip. "Yeah," he agreed, sleepily.

Without realizing what I was doing, my hand reached up and started playing with his hair. The silver color of it was fading again. That was the problem with colored hair—it faded so quickly. Silver suited him though.

"That feels good," he murmured. Then, suddenly, his eyes opened. "Oh," he said, pulling away from me.

With no covers and no heat from his body, I shivered. "Did you sleep OK?" I asked him.

He nodded, slowly, then turned away. "Sorry."

I shook my head. "Don't be sorry. I told you it was OK, and if it wasn't, then I wouldn't have let you stay."

He chewed at his lip, still not meeting my eyes. "I can't sleep by myself."

"You don't need to give me an explanation," I told him. "You can, but you don't need to. Not if you're not comfortable."

He didn't say anything. There was the briefest nod of his head, and then he got up, leaving me alone.

I washed and dressed quickly. I'd organized Kyun's appointment with the doctor early enough that we could join the others at their afternoon performance if he was given the all clear. H3RO, once again, would stick to the schedule as a foursome.

I made my way into the kitchen and grabbed some toast, not feeling particularly hungry. I was spreading on the peanut butter when Jun sauntered over and snatched half the toast from me. I backhanded his arm, but he grinned at me while eating the toast. "Good job I didn't want that," I grunted at him.

"Food always tastes better when it's shared with others," he told me.

I narrowed my eyes. "I'm not sure that's classed as sharing," I said, trying to work out why he was currently giving me a very weird look. "And on an unrelated matter, this morning—that really wasn't what it looked like."

"I'm not sure that is unrelated, but whatever," Jun said with a shrug. "And like I said earlier, I don't care if it is what it looks like." He tilted his head, as though considering his words, then shook it. "Actually, I care a little. But it's OK. I'll get my turn later." He reached over, squeezed my butt, then stole what was left of my toast before sauntering off.

"Jun!" I yelled after him. He was an annoying little maknae. Grumbling to myself, I stuck another slice of bread in the toaster, waiting for it to toast, then spread more peanut butter on it. I was pulling a bottle of orange juice from the fridge when I found Dante eating my breakfast. "Did Minhyuk not feed you guys this morning?" I grumbled, irritated.

"You make me hungry," he said, before giving me a smirk.

I closed my eyes, hoping I was conveying annoyance rather than the fact my body was suddenly humming from the memory of me and him and the six-course Michelin-starred Chinese meal. "I'm always hungry," he added.

My eyes flew open and I found him walking away, fist-bumping Nate as he made an appearance in the kitchen. I leaned back against the counter, my appetite completely gone and replaced with an even bigger knot of guilt. I'd been so caught up in Kyun and Tae for the last twenty-four hours that I hadn't given the whole 'what the hell was I doing?' situation a second thought.

"Is everything OK?" Nate asked me.

I nodded, even though it wasn't. There were some things that could be helped by talking to others, and maybe this was one of them, but seeing as Nate was one of the reasons my stomach was in a knot, this was probably one of the things I couldn't share with him. Maybe later I would call Kate. I'm sure she'd have some choice words about my situation, but she might be the voice of reason I needed. "You need to be leaving," I told him as Kyun appeared. "As do we."

제15 장

H3RO

Way Back Home

For obvious reasons, the doctor wouldn't share much of what he spoke to Kyun about with me. He however, did confirm that a lighter schedule would help, but as promotions were coming to an end, if Kyun felt he could handle it, then it was his call. Of course, that came with two conditions. He wanted to prescribe Kyun with some anti-anxiety medication, and he also wanted to meet with him a couple of times a week.

I had no objection to that, spending some time with the doctor's secretary to work out how we could fit this around H3RO's schedule. I was filled with a mixture of worry and relief. Worry that there was something upsetting Kyun, but relief that he was finally being given some of the support he clearly needed.

Kyun was quiet on our ride back to the dorm. The whole process had taken a lot more out of him than we'd anticipated. I made the executive decision that Kyun would have one last day of relaxation, especially as the afternoon show had already been briefed that it might just be four members of H3RO participating.

Kyun disappeared straight into his room, so I did the same in mine. Crazy as it sounded, I needed to get some laundry done and this was a perfect opportunity. I'd checked my emails then was about to empty the small laundry hamper to sort, when there was a knock at my door. "Come in," I called to Kyun, getting to my feet.

"Did you mean what you said?" he asked me.

I frowned, certain he'd asked me this before. "I'm not sure what you're referring to, but yes," I said with a shrug.

Kyun chewed at his lip, then, without meeting my eyes, pulled something out of his pocket, handing it over. I took it, frowning at the envelope, before realizing this was what he had slipped into his pocket a few nights previously. I pulled the letter out and my blood ran hot.

Fat piggy.
You bring H3RO down.
Just accept no one wants you.
No one will ever find you attractive.
Kill yourself now.

My fingers curled around the paper. Without a word, I stormed out of my room, marching to the kitchen, ready to head straight to Atlantis. This was too far. Fuck security, I was going straight to the legal team and I was going to find out exactly what I needed to do to press charges. In fact, fuck that idea all together, I was going to get security to find out who had written this, and I was going to deal with them myself.

I opened the door. Or I started to.

Suddenly, Kyun's arm shot out, slamming it shut. "Move out of the way," I growled, pulling at the door again. Once more, Kyun slammed it shut. I whirled around and found him right behind me.

"Where are you going?" he asked. He was staring at me, but his expression, other than serious, was unreadable.

"To commit murder," I told him through gritted teeth. "If you think I'm going to read this bullshit," I held the letter up to make my point, "And do nothing about it, you are very much mistaken, Kyun."

"You're shaking," he observed.

"I'm furious," I corrected him.

His other hand reached for my fist, wrapping around it and the letter. "Why?"

"I can't believe you have to ask that! It would be bad enough if it was just the bullshit about you being unattractive, but it's not!" I cried. "Kyun, this person is telling you to kill yourself! Of course I'm going to be furious. You have been carrying this around for days. This isn't even anything to do with me being your manager anymore—this has upset *me*." The last words came out as a sob. "It's not even about me and it's upsetting me, and I can't bear to think how much this is upsetting you."

Kyun's eyes darkened, then, using the hand he was holding onto, he pulled me to him, almost smashing his lips against mine.

He took a step forward, pressing his body against mine, then another, pushing us both back into the door with just enough force to make me gasp. His tongue darted in mine, his hand pushing mine up against the door. I dropped the letter. His kiss wasn't soft or teasing. It was raw and almost desperate. With my free hand, I clutched at his collar, pulling him close to me, even though, with him pressing me up against the door, there wasn't much closer he could get unless he removed his shirt.

With that idea flashing through my mind, I decided to do just that, struggling slightly with my one hand. He finally released my other hand, and I brought it in to help the other out making short work of his buttons.

As I pushed the shirt from his shoulders, his hands dropped to my butt, cupping it and picking me up. I wrapped my legs around him, gasping as his hardness rubbed against my soft core.

Somehow, with me clinging onto him, his tongue still attacking mine in a way which had me clawing at the back of his neck, he got us both into his bedroom. I wasn't sure how—I was already drunk on his frantic kisses—but he got us both on the bed. At the last minute, his hands left me to brace us before he fell on me.

The motion was enough for him to break away. He hovered above me, breathing heavily, his eyes filled with desire. "I want you so much," he told me, his voice raspy.

I wasn't sure what was driving this, and even though, somewhere in the back of my mind, there was a small voice telling me this might not be the best idea, I didn't care. I reached up and pulled him back to me with a little more force than was necessary. Then we were kissing each other, hard and rough.

There was a brief pause while he grabbed the hem of my dress, pulling it over my head and then flinging it across the room. My underwear soon followed. Then his jeans—and I discovered he wasn't wearing any underwear.

I stared at him in a lusty haze, drinking in every inch of him. He might not have been ripped, but he was gorgeous. A small, yet surprising discovery was that Kyun also had a tattoo. This was the first time I'd seen him without a shirt on. Even when swimming, he'd keep a (usually) black t-shirt on, so I'd never spotted it before: just above his nipple, over his heart, was 'H3RO'.

"I need you in me," I told him, not caring how desperate I sounded. When he jumped off the bed, I nearly panicked, but he stalked over to his drawers and yanked them open. While I stared at his butt, committing the dimples to memory, he rolled on a condom.

He turned back and gave me a look which had me squirming with need. He stalked back to the bed, standing over me. I wasn't sure if he was waiting for permission or not, but then he lunged at me, his hands pulling me to him. He lifted me slightly, parting my legs, and then he entered me with one rough thrust.

I cried out, my body not quite expecting his width, but enjoying the sensation at the same time. It was like a switch had been flicked and the last shred of control disappeared for both of us. My hands clawed at his back. His tongue fought with mine for dominance. Then he pulled out, almost all the way before he gave another rough thrust. I moved my mouth from his, unable to kiss him due to an unbearable need to shout his name.

His mouth moved to my neck and shoulders. Alternating between bites and kisses. Then he pulled almost all the way out again, hovering so he was just inside me. How he had the control, I had no idea. My body arched up, trying to draw him back in.

It worked, and he thrust in once more, harder. Then again. And again. Each time rough and hard, filling every available inch of me. His movements became faster and then he hit that sweet spot and I was done, crying out his name in a haze of pleasure.

A few thrusts after that and he was biting down on my shoulder in his own orgasm. My hands pulled him onto me as he collapsed with a welcome weight. We lay like that for a while, catching our breath, then he shifted so his weight was half off me. "That wasn't how I imagined that happening," he told me. His hand reached out, tracing a spot on my shoulder. "I'm sorry."

"I'm not," I said, reaching up to brush his hair out of his face so I could see his eyes better. "Though this wasn't quite what I had in mind when I said you could sleep with me."

Kyun sat up, reaching for the blanket. He brought it up, covering us both up. "I know," he said, quietly as he lay back down. "I'm sorry."

"Stop apologizing," I told him, firmly. I closed my eyes and stretched out my legs, intertwining them with his. "I feel so good right now," I added with a smile.

When Kyun's hand started tracing at my shoulder again, I opened my eyes and found him staring at me. "I'm struggling to believe it," he said, quietly.

"What?" He shook his head. "What?" I pressed, gently.

He kept his gaze firmly on my shoulder. "Don't laugh."

"I won't," I promised him.

His hand stilled. "How you think I'm one of the

most handsome guys you've seen," he mumbled.

It took me a moment to work out what he was saying, and then I moved my head forcing him to look at me. "Kyun, I meant it: I think you are beautiful."

"But I'm not—"

I reached up and pressed my fingers over his lips. "I don't care that you're not whoever you're about to compare yourself to. You're Kyun. And Kyun is hot as hell. And it's not just your looks, either. You're like a box of riddles that I want to work out, but the bits I've seen so far are just as wonderful. The only thing I want to change about you is your self-confidence, but I'm going to work on that," I promised him.

"I'm not sure I'm worth it," Kyun mumbled, once again diverting his gaze away. "I know I have a short temper, and I know I'm not easy to be around. I'm not warm like Minhyuk, or funny like Nate. I don't have the mental strength of Tae or the physical strength of Dante and—"

"Stop comparing yourself," I instructed him. "You're Kyun." I leaned over and kissed him. Unlike our previous kisses, this one was gentle, reassuring. I felt him sigh against me, then he shifted his weight, lifting himself up for a better angle.

Finally, he pulled away. "I know I haven't shown it, but I really am happy and grateful that you're in my life, Holly. I wish we could just stay here like this and not worry about anyone else outside this room." He frowned. "Although I do share this bed with Tae."

I think I felt my heart stop, and the little bubble popped.

Tae.

Jun.

Dante.

Nate.

Minhyuk.

And now, Kyun.

With all the calm I could muster, I fixed Kyun a smile. "Speaking of Tae, I need to go get him from the hospital." I slid out of the bed, then while trying to look like I wasn't about to bolt out of there, I gathered my things together and slipped out of the room. I darted to the bathroom, pulling the door closed behind me and hurried for a shower, all while attempting not to have a panic attack.

What. The. Hell. Was. I. Doing?

Six.

Six guys.

Six guys in the same group.

Six guys in the same group who shared the same dorm.

The *entire* group.

Who did that?

The knot in my stomach seemed to triple in size, and I doubled over, gasping for air. I couldn't keep doing this. It wasn't fair to any of them. I couldn't stand the guilt that was eating me alive from the inside out. I needed to stop this, before someone, or everyone got hurt.

H3RＯ

I spent longer in the bathroom than I should have, but I was close to having a panic attack. In the end, to allow myself to breathe again, I had come to the conclusion that telling Kate was not going to happen, she would either applaud me or cuss me out (neither of which I wanted). Coming clean wasn't the right option either: that might ease my guilt, but I was sure it would hurt everyone else. They didn't deserve that.

When I came out, Kyun was already dressed and waiting for me. I crouched down to collect the letter that had fallen to the floor earlier. "What are you doing with that?"

"I'm not going to go on a murder spree," I sighed. "But I am taking this to Atlantis later, because I am not allowing this to go undealt with. It's disgusting." I stood and turned to him. "If you ever read anything like this, or anything else that upsets you, I want to know." As Kyun nodded, I slipped the letter into my purse. "You're a part of H3RO, Kyun."

He nodded again, giving me a tight smile. I said goodbye and left to go to the office by myself: I had been serious about him taking the afternoon off and had made him promise he wouldn't go to the dance studio, but instead would actually relax.

I was seething inside. Kyun was, understandably, upset by this. I knew it wasn't the first time he'd had letters like this. And Atlantis had never done anything about it. I was barely a block away from the dorm when my phone rang. It was the hospital. They wanted to push Tae's discharge until mid-morning tomorrow as a crowd had formed outside and they were understandably concerned about the safety of their staff.

I rubbed at my forehead but agreed. It wasn't like he was being held in a prison—it was a hospital. It was warm and safe … but it wasn't home. I was sure he wanted to be back at the dorm because I knew the others, myself included, wanted him back. I agreed to a discharge time the following morning when a lot of the fans *should* be at school and promised that I would be there with security.

I sighed, the feeling of exhaustion settling in again. This was one group and Lee Woojin had plans for me taking a more senior position at Atlantis Entertainment where I would be responsible for more groups? It was a good job, despite how tired I was, I enjoyed what I was doing. But could I manage more of it? Once more, I found myself wondering how on earth an English Lit graduate was in this position.

제16 장

H3RO

Just That Little Thing

I marched into Lee Sejin's office and slammed the letter on his desk. He looked up at me, irritation radiating from him. "I don't care how many apology letters you write me, I'm not going to like you."

"What am I writing *you* an apology letter for?" I asked, curling my lip up in a sneer.

Sejin looked at me like I was a tramp who had walked in off the street. "Your existence would be a good start."

I looked around the room in confusion before looking back to him. "Oh, did I walk into the nursery? My bad." I leaned forward resting my hands on his desk. "I don't understand you," I told him, getting back on track. "How can you, as the Vice Chairman, as the person in charge of the welfare of the idols at Atlantis, do so little to protect one of the groups?"

Sejin rolled his eyes at me. "You're talking about H3RO again, aren't you?"

"Who else would I be talking about?" I asked him in disbelief. "What other group are you screwing over?"

"See, this is why women do not belong in a

corporate environment: they get so emotionally charged at things they know so little about."

"Oh, hell no!" I exclaimed. "Do not start with that sexist bullshit, or I will kick your ass."

"Please do," Lee Sejin said with a sickly-sweet tone. He leaned back in his chair, allowing his fingertips to temple together in front of him. "Please do."

"I see what you're trying to do, Sejin, and much as I would like to punch you in the face, with my Range Rover, I'm not going to allow you the satisfaction of having me arrested," I told him, evenly. "But I am going to do everything I can to see that you face some form of consequence for your actions—or lack thereof."

"Are you threatening me?" he scoffed.

I shrugged. "Why don't you wait and find out?"

"You hurt me, and you hurt Atlantis," Sejin told me like he was untouchable. "You hurt Atlantis and your precious H3RO will be the first to suffer."

I narrowed my eyes. "Do *not* underestimate me, Sejin," I told him, my hands balling into fists. "Or do? Whatever. Honestly, I don't care." I shrugged, with a dry laugh. I was done talking to this man. I snatched up the letter and left him, pausing at Park Inhye's desk outside. I started to open my mouth, ready to ask her a question, but shook my head. "Don't worry," I said instead to her worried face. "I know who your boss is. It doesn't matter."

I wandered down the corridor, lost in thought. Before I knew where I was, I was outside of Lee Woojin's office. I stared at his door, then, ignoring his secretary's objections (he really had to hate me at this point), I knocked and walked in.

Woojin looked up from the computer, his

irritation turning to confusion. "Holly? How can I help you?"

I stared at him, chewing at my lip. He waited patiently for me to speak. Finally, I did. "When you spoke to me before," I gestured to his office. "About this place: Atlantis. Were you telling me the truth, or were you telling me what you thought I wanted to hear?"

"I want you at this company," he said evenly, meeting my gaze.

I stared into his eyes, trying to see if he was lying or telling the truth. Physically, they looked so much like Lee Sejin's, it was hard, at first, to be certain. Yet, the more I stared, the more I saw the warmth and the hope. "I can't call you dad, and if I'm honest, I'm not sure I will ever be able to do that, but if you *were* serious about me and my place here at Atlantis, I can call you Chairman." I wrapped my arms around myself, feeling out of place.

Woojin glanced at his watch. "It's a little early, but I skipped lunch. Would you like to join me for something to eat?"

I eyed him suspiciously. "Are you going to sit me at a table with the rest of the family?"

"If at this moment, you are only capable of a business relationship, then let's keep it to that. Family can stay out of it," he responded.

"And what if the business part relates to Sejin or Seungjin?" I asked, dubiously.

"Then we will address it as if we were discussing any other employee at Atlantis," he said, calmly.

I wasn't sure how much I could keep family out of things when I had an asshole of a half-brother, but I nodded my head. "Where did you have in mind?"

"Somewhere close."

Close was the Atlantis canteen. It never occurred to me that the place would have one, but it made sense. There were a couple of hundred staff here, as well as all the idols and actors who came and went. Seeing as the building housed the dance studios, the recording studios, and a half-dozen other types of studios that were always open for the idols, there were always people here. Which meant they would need feeding.

What *really* surprised me was Woojin. He knew each of the servers by name and greeted them all personally. He didn't go so far as to introduce me to them as his daughter, but he did introduce them. We were given a large bowl of tteokbokki—spicy rice cakes.

At the back of the canteen was a raised area. There weren't that many tables, but they were all empty. Woojin led us to one of them and took a seat. How I had no idea this place existed until now showed me how much I walked around with blinkers. Aside from the view of the canteen, on the other side this area looked down on the main entrance area so by sitting here, we could see people coming and going from the building.

"That is Park Chang Soo," Woojin told me, pointing to a ridiculously good-looking man as he walked in the building. "Currently filming 'Love or Luxury'." He took a bite of his tteokbokki and smiled appreciatively at his bowl. "The chef knows just how to make this," he said. "Park Changsoo has just finished his military enlistment and he is more popular than when he went in." He pointed at a woman. "That's Ha Moonhee," he continued. "She's been modelling with us for nearly ten years. She wanted to be an idol but unfortunately, was unable to overcome her stage fright."

"Just being able to list a few names isn't going to prove anything to me," I said, watching him carefully. I was wary, to say the least.

"You said you wanted to discuss business," he shrugged.

"And when I become President, then I will make sure I learn the entire Atlantis Entertainment roster—all the groups, solo artists, actors and models—but right now, I'm just H3RO's manager. Right now, they are my priority."

"Aim higher, Holly," Woojin said, simply.

My eyes widened in disbelief. "If you are going to start insulting H3RO, we can end lunch now," I told him as I got to my feet.

"Vice Chairwoman, not just President," he elaborated. He looked up at me and tilted his head. "And you're not *just* H3RO's manager. From what I can see, you're taking charge of marketing and promotions, security, and health, to name but a few positions."

"You know?" I asked, sitting back down. That surprised me. "Then why have you been sitting there, watching me fuck it all up?"

"I wish you wouldn't use such vulgar language," he chided me. "And to answer your question," he continued as I pulled a face. "People learn best when they make mistakes. That hard lesson is often the best lesson. You have made a few slips along the way, but there was nothing I would class as a *fuck up*. What's more, you've never asked for help until now."

"I haven't?" I asked in disbelief. "Do you know how many times I have been in this building asking for help? I was told to get H3RO a comeback, and I couldn't even find anyone who would tell me the process to make a single."

"You found out though," Woojin said.

I sighed, rubbing at my temples. "Well, I'm asking for help now."

Woojin nodded. "What with?"

My hands came to rest on the table, either side of my untouched bowl of tteokbokki. I started tapping at the table while I sent a silent prayer that I wasn't about to make a mistake. "Where do you really stand with H3RO being disbanded?" I asked, curious, my plea for help dependent on his answer.

"I believe your agreement with Sejin was that H3RO would deliver two number one singles. I am still waiting on the second, but they do need to get through their current promotions."

That translated to: he wasn't set on seeing them be disbanded. *Yet.*

"And you meant what you said about wanting to help artists?" I asked.

Woojin nodded. "*That* is imperative."

I pulled the letter from Kyun's anti-fan out of my purse and set it on the table in front of Woojin's bowl. Silently, Woojin leaned over, his eyes scanning the page. "Kyun received this. It's not the first one he's received over the years."

"Mail should be vetted in the mailroom before it's delivered to an artist," Woojin said, glancing up at me. "This must not have been delivered here?"

I shook my head. "I had a dozen or so boxes of fan mail delivered to my office the other day. This was in one of the boxes I took back to the dorm for them.

Had I known, I would have sat and checked everything first."

"That is not your job, and the mailroom should be doing that automatically. We employ a team specifically for that," Woojin informed me, looking displeased at my revelation.

"And yet they're not. *I* had a letter sent to me," I said, pulling out the letter in question. Woojin took it off me, his expression growing darker. "This was around the time of the article."

"This is unacceptable," he growled, slamming the letter down. "Sejin—"

"Sejin couldn't care less if he tried," I cut him off. "He doesn't like me: he wants me out. He doesn't like H3RO: he wants them out. I told him we'd had things thrown at us and he brushed it off. He might be good at making this company money, but he does it at the expense of his artists."

"I am going to take these to the security team and deal with this," Woojin said, gathering up the two letters.

"They already have them, along with a dozen others I pulled out of the pile of boxes in my office," I said with a dismissive wave of my hand. "They also have countless screenshots of the malicious comments on the SNS. If you're going to do anything, I would suggest talking to the legal team, because they refuse to file charges unless Sejin signs off on it. Which he hasn't."

Woojin's jaw hardened. I watched as a small vein began pulsing at his temple. "You and H3RO are employees of Atlantis Entertainment. Regardless of his opinion on any of you, his responsibility is to look after our employees." Each word was clipped. I had a feeling my temper may have come from these genes. "I will see to it this is escalated. Thank you for coming to me about this."

"I shouldn't have had to, Woojin," I told him, trying hard not to scoff at the man who was actually going to help me. "You said you would give me additional power. I'm not after shares, and I don't want Sejin's job: I have my own. I want to be able to do that. I want to be able to protect my guys from crap like this before it gets to them, and when I can't, I want to be able to send a message to all the crazy anti-fans that this behavior is unacceptable."

"Sejin is not a naturally nasty man, Holly," Woojin sighed. "He should have done something when this started."

I folded my arms and fixed the man opposite me a firm stare. "Tae is in a hospital right now, because he broke his arm trying to stop something that was launched at us from hitting me. Do you think that's when it started? Because it's not. It's not even when Jun and I were walking back from here one night, and some crazy girl decided to throw an egg at the back of my head. This goes back further: Kyun has had so many nasty things said about him since he debuted that I'm actually worried about his mental health. That's *years* of Lee Sejin not doing things for H3RO."

"Sejin's attention may have lapsed on occasion, but I can't believe that he would intentionally allow for things to become as physical as that, regardless of his feelings towards H3RO. I refuse to believe that he would have allowed malicious comments directed at Ha Kyun Gu to continue had he known what was happening," Woojin returned. His anger had eased off, but he still looked displeased with my accusations.

I decided not to push it. Our relationship, our business relationship, was on new, shaky ground. I'd already accomplished something by getting him to speak to the legal team. Whatever he said about keeping business and family separate, Lee Sejin was not only his son, he was his firstborn. It would take some time to remove those blinkers. Assuming that would ever be possible.

I would have plenty of battles to fight if I stayed here. If I wanted to outlast Sejin, or at least see him suffer some form of consequence for his actions (or lack of), then I needed to outlast him, and that meant knowing when to keep going, and when to bow out. I took a few bites of my tteokbokki. It was good. I mean, it was now cold, but the canteen was somewhere I would be happy coming back to.

"Sponsorship."

I looked at Woojin in confusion. "Excuse me?"

"A group doesn't just earn money from their album sales. They can increase their income with sponsorship," Woojin explained.

I knew that. That was why I had gone to Dante when the underwear designer wanted to have him model for them. When the mental image of Dante in the underwear … and out of the underwear … popped up in my head, I nearly choked on my rice cake. That wasn't quite the thing to be thinking about in front of your father, regardless how pleasing an image it was.

"Despite the success H3RO have had recently, there hasn't been much in the sponsorship department," I sighed.

Woojin's eyes narrowed. "They had a number one

single." I nodded, puzzled. "They're an Atlantis Entertainment group," he elaborated. I just nodded again, still confused by this line of discussion. Woojin sighed patiently. "Holly, I would have expected at least one brand—whether that be clothing, shoes, food or cosmetics—to be in touch wanting to sponsor H3RO. I find it quite strange no one has."

I raised my shoulders, at a loss. "I'm always on my emails, checking the spam folder, I check the SNS several times a day, my phone is always with me and never off. Woojin, with the exception of someone wanting Dante to model for them, *no one* has been in touch with me regarding any kind of sponsorship."

Woojin shook his head. "Your secretary—"

My burst of laughter sounded like a snort. "Secretary? I don't have one of those!"

"You should have," he said, slowly.

"Well if I have, we've never been introduced."

Once again, Woojin looked displeased. "I will see to it that is rectified also."

My eyes widened. "Can I choose?"

"Of course. You should have someone you can trust."

"What if this person is already employed in the company. Can I find out what they're on and beat the salary?"

"You have someone in mind?" he asked, surprised.

I nodded, eagerly. "Yes."

"If you trust them, make the offer," he shrugged.

I could feel the biggest grin take over my face. I knew exactly where I was going next.

제17 장

H3R오

Boom Boom

P ark Inhye gaped at me with her mouth wide open. "Me?" she finally asked.

"If there's one person in this company I trust, it's you," I nodded. "Lee Woojin has given his blessing to beat whatever money Lee Sejin is currently paying you."

"I'd take a pay cut," she muttered, leaning over to grab her purse from out of the bottom drawer. While I sat on her desk, watching her with raised eyebrows, she swept the items on the top of her desk into her purse. Then she moved onto emptying some of the items from her drawers. "I'll go get settled in," she declared, marching off down the hallway while I watched her go.

"OK then," I muttered, amused. I was expecting to have to negotiate a little. No, that was a lie. I was expecting her to accept: I knew what she thought of my half-brother. I just wasn't expecting her to relocate *that* quickly. I followed after her. "I won't lie to you, Inhye," I sighed. "I've been doing this by myself. I have no idea what I'm doing, and I have no idea what state things are in if I'm entirely honest. Lee Woojin seems to think there should be sponsorship offers for H3RO, but I've never seen one, and I wouldn't know where to start."

Inhye gaped up at me. "Forget that pay cut. I want a pay raise."

"Done."

"And sick pay."

"OK," I shrugged.

Inhye smiled, then sighed. "Sick pay isn't legally required in this country," she told me. "You really don't know what you're doing, do you?"

"Nope," I admitted. "But you can have sick pay as far as I'm concerned."

"I will start by getting things organized. Please give me access to your calendars." I nodded. "And please give me a few days to work out where we are and where I think the gaps are."

I walked into my office feeling much better. Everything was finally settling down.

Most things were finally settling down.

There was still something I needed to address.

Six somethings.

I walked over to the window and frowned. How long could I put off having a conversation with each of them?

I glanced back at the pile of boxes that remained in my office. Well, a couple more hours, at least …

I pulled a box over to my desk and resumed where I'd left off. Like last time, most letters were sweet. Once again, however, there were some questionable messages in there, though none were anywhere near as awful as what Kyun had received.

I reached for the next envelope. This one was a little bulky, like there was something in it. I slit it open and poured the contents on my desk. It was fabric.

Weird. I prodded the black lacy material with my pen, and then I realized what it was.

Panties.

Used panties.

I dropped the pen and leaped away from my desk as quickly as I could, thoroughly revolted.

I darted out of my office, looking for Inhye but there was no one there. It was only then that I realized how late it was. Feeling nauseous, I used her phone to request someone come to remove them, only half joking when I suggested they wear a hazmat suit.

Who did that?

Seriously? Who thought that sending used panties was a good idea.

I shuddered, too icked out to go back in the room.

"Planning a career change?" Nate asked, laughing.

From behind Inhye's desk, I looked over, finding him and one of the members of Onyx, JongB watching me. The fact these two were friends didn't surprise me. They were both rappers, both American-Korean, and both a similar age. Nate had told me when he first joined Atlantis he had struggled with his Korean. I'd have sought out another American if I could, too.

"Yeah, being a manager is just too stressful," I sighed, flopping onto the desk.

JongB chuckled. He was one of those people with an infectious laugh: it was loud and actually sounded like *ha ha ha.* "If I was your manager, I would have quit months ago," he told Nate.

Nate snorted. "If I was *your* manager, I'd have fired your ass months ago. You're more annoying than Jun."

"Hey!" JongB objected. "No one is more

annoying than Jun!"

Nate and JongB shared a look. "Kyungwon!" they cried together, before fist-bumping.

I sat up, shaking my head in amusement, vaguely recognizing the name as a member of B.W.B.B. "I needed to call a hazmat team into my office," I told them.

The pair stopped and turned, their eyes wide. "Why?" JongB asked, looking thrilled, as though there was a scandal about to break.

"Fangirls."

A small smirk appeared on Nate's face. "Now, I know this body is fine," he raised the bottom of his t-shirt and flashed me his abs. He wasn't wrong … "But you don't have to murder fangirls because it's all yours."

"Bro!" JongB exclaimed in mock disgust. "Don't flirt with your manager like that. And put them away!" he swiped at Nate's stomach, making him drop the t-shirt. "No one wants to see that."

Nate's eyes met mine as the knot of guilt tightened in my stomach. Even JongB thought it was inappropriate to flirt with me—and he didn't know what was going on between us. I mean, I didn't know what was going on between us, but I knew what *had* happened.

"Why are you guys here this late?" I asked, trying to change the subject.

"We came to take you dancing," Nate told me.

"Huh?"

"You said you wanted a night of drinking and dancing," Nate shrugged. "JongB and I were going to hit up a club in Hongdae, and we're bringing you with us."

"You want to bring your manager to a club?" I asked, dubiously.

"It's not like you're an old manager," JongB shrugged. That earned him a smack to the gut from Nate. "Well, she's not!" he objected. He turned back to me. "Plus, we get the added bonus of no one will tell us off because we have management with us."

"How do you know I won't tell you off?" I asked him.

"Nate said you're cool. I trust him," JongB shrugged.

"I'm not sure I feel like going to a club," I sighed, frowning. "Not after the last one."

"We're not going to that kind of club," Nate promised me.

JongB looked between us both with his eyes wide. "What kind of club did you two go to last time?"

"It's just going to be a night of dancing," Nate continued, ignoring JongB whose mind I was sure was going crazy with theories. "Come on!" he said, nodding his head in the direction of the exit.

"My purse," I frowned.

"JongB?" Nate said, looking at the younger rapper, expectantly.

Before I could stop him, JongB had run into the office. Moments later there was a squeal which sounded far too high-pitched for the guy who had just run in. It was followed up his loud *ha ha ha*'s, the sound of running footsteps, and then JongB burst out of the door. "Who were they addressed to?"

My nose wrinkled up. "Please tell me you didn't touch them?"

"Touch what?" Nate asked, looking half amused

and half puzzled.

"SOMEONE SENT H3RO UNDERWEAR!" JongB bellowed before doubling over with his laughter echoing around us.

Nate arched an eyebrow at me. "Used," I clarified. "Hence the need for hazmat."

"Who sent them?" Nate asked as JongB almost staggered over to me, handing me my purse.

"Your mom," JongB sniggered, ducking out of the way of Nate's fist.

I bit back my smile. "I'm not sure going to a club is a good idea," I told Nate.

"You said you needed a night of dancing," Nate shrugged. "So, you're going to get one. No arguments. Let's go."

"You have a show tomorrow morning," I pointed out.

"You cancelled it because Tae is being discharged from the hospital," Nate countered. "And I've done plenty of shows with no sleep. Hungover too."

I fixed him an unimpressed look. "You think that's an argument that's going to convince me?"

"Hey!" Nate held his hands up. "I am a young guy and I drink. But tonight, I won't." JongB snorted. "Fine," he said, shooting JongB a withering glare. "I will only have a few beers. You said you wanted to go out dancing. I want to go out dancing. He wants to be annoying and tag along," he added, jabbing his thumb in JongB's direction. "And how much trouble can I get into with my manager present?"

I sat back in Inhye's chair. The idea of going out and letting my hair down was appealing. But, I was tired.

Then again, being tired meant going back to the

dorm.

And that meant facing the others.

OK, I was being a chicken, but the idea of sitting in the same room as all of them, knowing I had kissed all of them (or more), was doing things to the knot in my stomach.

Tonight, I would go out, dance, relax, maybe have a little liquid courage, and then I would at least speak to Nate. That was reasonable, right? "Fine," I conceded. I gathered up my purse and followed Nate and JongB to the elevator. "Where are we going?" I asked when he didn't press the button for the ground floor.

"Getting changed," he shrugged.

I had no idea what he was scheming, but as I was willing to bet, what with the look in his eyes, he wouldn't tell me even if I asked. I was led to a room where an extraordinarily pretty girl with short hair and pixie-like features was waiting. "Hi Nari," JongB greeted the leader of Cupcake.

"What's going on?" I asked. "Are you about to go all 'Princess Diaries' on me?"

Nate shook his head. "Nah. Nari just agreed to lend you a dress."

"Welcome to our wardrobe," she said, waving her hand behind her at the rows upon rows of clothing. "You two can get out now," she added before ushering Nate and JongB from the room.

"What's with all the clothes?"

"We got a few sponsorship deals over the years, and gifts of clothes," Nari explained. "When we were in the smaller dorm, we couldn't fit them all there so we would store them here. When we moved, we took all the ones we loved and cycled these out." She was

168

already walking to a rack, browsing through it. "Here," she said, handing a dress over.

I looked at the dress she was holding up. It wasn't what I would normally have chosen, covered in large printed flowers, but it was really pretty. I took it off her and tried it on. The cut was my style, and it was comfortable. I gave a twirl in the mirror, watching the skirt flare out. "I like it," I declared.

"It's all yours," she shrugged. "I wasn't sure if you were planning on going back to the dorm. Nate was talking about him and JongB getting ready here. We've been in the dance studio all afternoon, so I assume not. I have my makeup with me if you want to borrow it?"

Her makeup bag was a small suitcase. Literally. She pulled it over and opened it up, then before I could stop her, she started handing me containers. I realized, as she helped me put the makeup on, much as I enjoyed living with guys, it was nice to have female company. Kate had gone back to America already. Maybe I needed to find a way to bring her back.

It didn't take long to finish. Although Nari was set on me wearing a beautiful but killer looking pair of heeled sandals, I decided to stick with the kitten heels I was already wearing. At least that way I would stand half a chance of surviving a night of dancing. I thanked her and then walked out to find Nate and JongB waiting.

JongB had left his currently blonde hair to fall naturally, covering most of his forehead, apart from a small sliver to the left. Nate's, still a shade of light brown, was swept to the side. Both were wearing dark jeans and a shirt. Atlantis Entertainment really did have some good-looking guys on their roster.

I could feel the heat from Nate's stare as his eyes

swept over me. *No*, I chided myself. *Tonight, I'm going to have a conversation with him, not sex.* A little voice in the back of my head was trying to convince me that both *could* be possible, but the knot in my stomach was winning out on that not happening.

I was about to reconsider my decision to go out, but I was led downstairs and into the back of an Uber. I sat in it, one side of me pressed up against the door, the other pressed up against Nate's muscular body. I tried to keep my attention on the world outside of the back of the car, but failed spectacularly. Although Nate wasn't doing anything to draw JongB's attention to us, I was sure he was sat in the middle with his legs spread a little wider than they needed to be. His arm, resting in his lap, was gently resting against mine.

I sucked in a deep breath: it was going to be a long night.

제18 장

H3R오

Black Out

The club was packed, but I realized most people didn't look twice at us. OK, so they weren't going to look twice at me, but JongB was in one of the most popular groups at the moment, and with H3RO's recent promotions, Nate carried his own level of popularity. Despite this, we were left to ourselves.

JongB led us to the bar, ordering himself and Nate a bottle of beer while I went for a glass of wine. I wasn't a big drinker, and I could sip this. With our drinks in our hands, JongB continued to lead us through the crowds to a quieter area at the back. It didn't say VIP anywhere, but it gave off that impression.

While Nate and JongB chatted away loudly over the volume of the music, I closed my eyes and listened to the EDM song that was playing. The beat was making my ribcage vibrate and I liked it. I wasn't a dancer, but I did like to dance. Swaying slightly to the music, I was glad I hadn't changed my mind and had allowed Nate to take me out.

"I told you it would be different to last time," Nate spoke loudly in my ear, making me open my eyes in surprise.

I looked at him and nodded. "I needed this," I admitted.

"But I think a repeat of what happened after would be a good idea," he said, moving in closer so he didn't have to shout. As though using that as an excuse, his hand settled on the small of my back.

I couldn't control the shiver of anticipation that ran through me, but I turned, stepping out of Nate's hold. "Nate," I sighed. "You are an idol, and you're out in public. You can't just be touching women, even if I am your manager. You don't need those photos all over SNS."

"I'm not touching any woman," he said, looking disappointed. "I'm touching you, and you should know that this is not how I intend on touching you later."

Before I could comment, JongB's head appeared between ours as he draped an arm around each of our shoulders. "Guys, this place is full of beautiful women." He looked at me. "OK, there might be some good-looking guys out there, but you're going to be hard-pressed to find any better looking than us: sorry, noona. But we should go dance. Or drink some more."

To hell with it.

I finished off my wine, ignored Nate's arched eyebrow, and deposited the wine glass on the side. Without a second thought, I walked down onto the dance floor and disappeared into the crowd. It didn't take long for Nate and JongB to join me.

Although the latter had mentioned the place being full of beautiful women, and it was, he was more content dancing with myself and Nate. Onyx were a relatively new group and I had a suspicion they also had a no-dating clause in their contract. I wouldn't have put that past Lee Sejin, although I begrudgingly had to admit, from a PR point of view, it made sense.

I stopped suddenly. *That*. I had an excuse to end things with everyone, and I could do it without telling them anything else. I sighed: no, that wouldn't work. These guys lived with each other. It was bound to come up in conversation eventually.

Although, that begged the question: why hadn't it already?

"Are you OK?" Nate asked, his concerned face appearing in my line of sight.

I blinked, focusing on him, and then nodded. "I need a drink."

"Good idea." Nate signaled to JongB we were heading to the bar, and then we left the dancefloor heading to the bar area. Although the volume of the music was quieter up here, it was still busy.

"I'm going to the bathroom," I called to them, before disappearing. I weaved through the crowds, finding the corridor to the bathroom. When I came back out, Nate was waiting for me. "I'm old enough to go to the bathroom alone," I said with half a smile.

"I thought women couldn't do that."

"I'm really a man," I joked.

Nate stepped up to me, the gap between us almost disappearing as he leaned in towards my ear. "Now, we both know that's not true," he murmured. Then he nipped at my earlobe.

At the sound of two girls walking drunkenly along the corridor towards us, Nate wrapped his arm around my waist, ducked his head, and led us further down the corridor past the bathroom.

My heart was already going a million miles a minute as he whirled me around in his arms. My hands went up to grab his large upper arms to steady myself. That wasn't a smart move: I couldn't stop my hands from rubbing over the toned muscles. I licked my lower lip before I could stop myself.

With his broad back hiding me from view, his hands tightened around my waist. He dipped his head, capturing my lips with his. His mouth was warm and familiar. Although I had seen him on a daily basis, my body melted against him like I hadn't seen him for months.

His hands slowly started moving from my hips, up my side, settling just under my bra. While one hand stayed there, holding me in place, the other curved round, cupping me. My back arched against him as I gasped from his touch, and then his tongue was in my mouth, massaging my own.

Then he pulled away, his mouth trailing kisses down my throat. I let out another moan of pleasure. He carefully started pulling the neckline to the dress, his mouth moving lower.

With willpower I'd thought had escaped me months ago, I managed to move my hand to his, pulling it back down and off my breast. We were in a club. He couldn't be doing this here. I was serious before: the last thing H3RO needed was a picture of me and Nate joining the one of me and Dante.

Dante … Jun … Kyun …

Before my brain could finish listing all the members of H3RO, Nate pulled away abruptly, fixing me a stare which had me suddenly questioning if I had said one of their names.

"What's that?" he asked.

"What's what?" I asked in return.

"Is that a bite mark?" he demanded.

I froze. "Yes." I had forgotten about that.

"I didn't do that."

"No," I agreed, my voice barely audible.

Nate stared down at me, his eyes dark and intense. I wasn't sure if he was going to go punch someone. "Who did this?"

I stared up at him, unable to look away, even though I didn't want to meet his stare. This was what I'd expected, which meant, when I told him who did it, the look I was going to get from him would break my heart.

Oh crap.

It was going to break my heart.

I liked him.

No, I think I was falling in love with him.

With them.

I dropped my head. "Kyun," I whispered.

"Kyun?" he repeated. "Really?"

I looked back at him with a frown, despite everything. "Don't say it like that," I told him.

Nate stepped back, holding his hands up. "I didn't mean it like that."

"Yet you sound surprised. Is that because he would sleep with me, or I would sleep with him."

Nate's eyes went wide. "You slept with him?"

Way to go Holly! There were maybe a hundred other ways with tact that I could have said that, but no. The cat was out of the bag now. Slowly I nodded.

Nate ran his tongue over his teeth, folding his arms as he stared at me. "For the record, my surprise comes at the fact Kyun is a biter. That's the kind of kink I expect from Dante, who, if I'm honest, is who I thought you might have slept with."

I stared up at him, speechless. I could hear his words, but they were making no sense. He thought I had slept with Dante? Yet minutes ago he had his hands all over me. "I haven't slept with Dante," I finally told him, still wondering if this was a weird hallucination.

Nate cocked his head, his eyes narrowing. "But you have done something with him."

It wasn't a question, but I nodded my head anyway. "Nate," I started.

Nate held his hand up, shaking his hand. "I can't believe he was right," he muttered, so quietly I barely heard him.

"Who?" I asked, carefully.

Nate shook his head, looking back at me. "He said it would be OK, but I'm not sure how I feel about this. I need to think."

Before I could ask him what he was talking about, he walked off, back into the club. I dropped to a crouch, wrapping my arms around my legs. Squeezing my body together as tightly as I could: I felt like I was about to fall to pieces and this was the only way to stop it happening.

"This is why you shouldn't have done something like this," I told my knees, miserably. I was sure the knot in my stomach had grown again. I felt sick, but I also felt empty. I had been selfish and wanted them all, and now I was going to be left with none.

But what if this also impacted H3RO? The agreement was I would be their manager and get them two number ones. I couldn't work with them now, could I? It wasn't because of the looks and comments I was going to get, although the thought of hate in any of their eyes brought tears to mine. It was because I couldn't be there knowing my presence was going to hurt them. They had no clue. I was the one who had done everything with my eyes wide open.

I stayed there in the corridor for a while, wallowing in self-pity. It was easier to stay and hide here than go and face Nate.

That was assuming he was still here and hadn't gone back to the dorm to tell the others.

My eyes widened and I shot to my feet. What if he had told the others?

I hurried back into the club, searching the dancefloor for Nate or JongB. I was almost in a blind panic as I tried to make my way back to where we had been seated, when JongB wrapped his arm around my wrist. "Holly!" he cried enthusiastically. "Where have you been?"

"Where's Nate?" I asked him, sure that if he was here, Nate was too.

"He's fine," he tried to assure me as he attempted to lead me to the dancefloor.

I came to a dead stop, JongB jerking back. He turned to me. "Where is he?" I asked.

JongB winced. "OK, I know what our contracts say, but please don't be too harsh on him."

I pulled my hand free and turned on my heel, marching back to the table we had been at. Sat behind it was Nate, and almost in his lap was an exceptionally pretty girl with wide eyes, a heart shaped mouth, and cleavage that made mine look like a pre-pubescent girl's.

"If you're going to tell anyone off, tell me off,"

JongB said, stepping in front of me and cutting off the view. "She came and asked me what he would drink and then I kinda pushed them together."

"How much has he had to drink?" I asked quietly, looking at the bottle of top branded vodka on the table. It was half empty.

"He came back from the bathroom and had a few shots, but they've been sharing that," JongB shrugged. "Nate can handle his liquor.

It wasn't whether or not he could handle his liquor, so much as how drunk was he? Despite everything, my heart was about to implode at the sight of this gorgeous woman, her leg crossed so her thigh was not only on show but draped over Nate's lap. She was leaning into him as he had his arm wrapped around her, and he could barely keep his head up to look at her face.

I had no right to be a jealous girlfriend, but I was torn between going over there and tearing her off him by her hair or running out of the club in tears. When she leaned closer to him, her hand slithering in his shirt through the gap between the buttons, while her mouth closed in on his, it looked like the second option was the resulting outcome.

When Nate's hand settled on her bare thigh, stroking absently back and forth, I couldn't take it anymore. I turned, trying to avoid JongB, and pushed my way through the club, outside into the fresh air. It was raining. Of course, it was. I moved out of the way of the main door, sheltering under a canopy as I tried to locate an Uber to pick me up.

Seeing as my luck was staying true, there were no available cars anywhere close. I sighed, wrapping my arms around me, keeping an eye out for a taxi.

"Did you really expect anything else?" I asked myself, bitterly.

Actually, yes, I did. I didn't expect Nate to jump on the next girl he could find, regardless of how stunning she was. Of all of them, not Nate. A lump formed in the back of my throat, and I had to use the back of my fist to wipe away the blurry vision I was experiencing. I was cold, and it wasn't because of the weather.

"Are you OK?"

I looked up at the tall guy in front of me and nodded. "Yes, thank you."

"You don't look OK," he disagreed. He glanced up at the rain, and then stepped under the canopy with me. I took a step back, trying to find my personal space, but he followed me. "Looks like I wasn't the only one to come out without a coat tonight."

"I'll be OK," I said, carefully. "My boyfriend will be out with my coat soon."

"Now, we both know you're lying," the man said, placing his arm on my shoulder.

You don't grow up in Chicago without learning a trick or two.

I reached up, grabbed his hand, sticking my nails into the fleshy area at the base of his thumb. I'm not particularly strong or big, but that was a move which took little energy and managed to bring the man to his knees as I bent his arm back. He let out a yell of pain. "When a girl tells you that she's waiting for her boyfriend, it's a polite way of saying she's not interested," I snapped at him, letting him go.

Irritated, I started to leave the dry patch of the

canopy to move onto the next one. Then a hand was on my wrist, yanking me back so hard, I thought my arm was going to pop out its shoulder.

"Get off her."

The man and I turned to find Nate standing just behind us. I stared at him. Something wasn't right. He was swaying slightly, and he didn't look like he was able to focus on anything properly. "This is none of your business, idol," the man sneered at him. "Run along and go look pretty somewhere else."

"It is my business when you're assaulting my girlfriend," Nate announced, although his words sounded slurred.

"Let's just all go home," I suggested.

The man turned back to me. I wasn't sure what he was going to do or say, but the next thing I knew, I could see Nate lunging at him. The man saw it too, stepping out of the way to avoid Nate's fist. I wasn't quick enough.

Nate's punch slammed me against the wall. I had never been hit before. I had no idea it would hurt this much. My cheek felt like it had been split open. I could taste blood. The tears started to mix with the rain that was splattering over my face. All I wanted to do was curl up in a ball.

"Holly!" Nate cried in horror, staggering over to me. He looked mortified, but at the same time, he couldn't stand straight. Behind us, the man ran off. I barely paid attention as Nate fell against me. Despite the pain I was in, I tried to keep him upright. "Holly, I didn't …" he slurred his words, blinking rapidly. "I don't feel right."

"What's going on?" I heard JongB yell, hurrying

over. Before my knees buckled, he was sliding under Nate's shoulder, bearing the weight for me.

"Something's not right," I told JongB, looking over at the crowd of people which were forming. Thankfully, because of the rain, it was small, but they still had their phones out. "Don't turn around," I told JongB. "We need to get out of here."

Nodding, JongB held Nate up so I could take his other side. Together, we tried to half-carry, half-drag him away from the club. "This isn't going to work," JongB muttered. With some effort, he maneuvered his body underneath Nate's to get him on his back. Although JongB was much slimmer than Nate, he managed to support his friend, carrying him down the street as fast as he could. "What happened to him? What happened to you?" he asked.

I jogged alongside them to keep up. "A guy started touching me, and Nate went to hit him, but he hit me instead."

"He hit you?" JongB asked in disbelief.

"Not intentionally," I stressed.

"OK, don't get mad, but Nate has been known to get into fights when he's drunk," JongB said.

My lips thinned into a line. "I've heard."

"It's not like that," JongB said, pausing to reposition Nate. "Nate will always help a damsel in distress. The point is, he's not a bad fighter: it's not like him to miss, much less hit someone else."

Something didn't feel right to me, either. I glanced behind us: we seemed to be far enough away from the club and thankfully no one had followed after us. "Over here," I said, beckoning JongB into a doorway.

He set Nate down and we watched as the rapper slumped to the side. "That's not alcohol, Holly."

I agreed. I pulled out my phone, praying for an Uber. Someone up there heard me, as the little car icon flashed up. Then I closed the app. I couldn't risk taking Nate to a hospital in an Uber. Instead I called the Atlantis security team. They promised a car was fifteen minutes out.

"What happened in there?" I demanded.

"I was going to ask the same thing," JongB returned.

I glanced down at Nate, then crouched beside him, pushing his head back. He was breathing, but he didn't seem conscious. I pushed an eyelid back and a hand gave a half-hearted attempt at pushing me away. He was conscious. His pupils didn't look right, though. "Did he take something?" I asked JongB.

The faux-blond shook his head. "Nate doesn't do drugs."

This wasn't just alcohol though. The wind blew down the street; as I was soaked, it was freezing. Nate being barely conscious in it wasn't good. I rubbed my hands up and down his arms, hoping it would help a little. If nothing else, it was giving me something to focus on before I burst into tears from worry.

Finally, the car arrived. The driver jumped out, running over to help move Nate into the back of the car. Blankets were draped over us, but I took mine off, wrapping it around Nate. I reached over, cranking the heat of the car up as high as it would go, continuing to rub at Nate as the driver took us to the nearest hospital.

제19 장

H3RO

Nightmare

I had forced JongB to take the car back to the dorm: there was no need for him to be at the hospital and the last thing he needed was that image over SNS. We exchanged numbers and I promised to let him know what was happening with Nate.

I waited by myself in a large, empty waiting room, pacing back and forth. It wasn't until a nurse came and gave me some blankets to wrap up in, that I realized how cold I was. I was completely soaked, and the hospital's air conditioning had my body covered in goosebumps. I hadn't noticed though, because I felt numb.

First Tae and now Nate. I couldn't shake the feeling that they were connected. What was worse, I couldn't shake the feeling that *I* was that connection. Both times they were with me, and both times they were trying to protect me. I was bad luck.

It was also yet another reason why I shouldn't be involved with them.

After almost an hour of nothing, a doctor finally approached me. "Miss Lee?"

I nodded, praying that the older woman was going to give me good news. "Yes?"

"We have run some blood tests and we've just got the results back. They're showing positive for flunitrazepam."

I stared blankly at her. "I don't know what that is."

"The other name for it is rohypnol."

"A roofie? Someone roofied Nate?" I exclaimed. At least his behavior made sense. "Why would someone roofie him?"

The doctor shook her head. "I could not tell you," she said, apologetically. "Flunitrazepam, often known as the date rape drug, is a sedative, as it affects the user's consciousness. It also impairs cognitive function, memory recall, and concentration."

"How is he?" I asked. *Why* wasn't important at the moment.

"The drug is leaving his system; however, I'm going to keep him in overnight, under observation. This is only precautionary, but I would rather he stay here."

I nodded, feeling dazed. Then I sank into one of the uncomfortable plastic bucket seats.

"Miss Lee, might I suggest you go home and get changed into something dry. There's nothing more you can do here, and he is sleeping now. Go home and get some rest yourself. We will look after him," she promised me.

I wasn't sure I would be able to sleep, but I nodded. JongB lived in the same building as H3RO, a couple of floors below. I had no doubt that he had gone straight to their dorm and let them know what had happened. I pulled out my phone, but the battery was dead. Wonderful.

With my limbs feeling like lead from the fatigue, I left the blanket with the nurses, then made my way to the exit. Thankfully, being a hospital, there were plenty of taxies around here. I grabbed one, slumping back in the seat as I stared out of the window. It was the time in the morning when the sun was just starting to make its way over the horizon. Everything was slowly getting lighter, but with the clouds in the sky, everything was gray.

I wasn't able to finish typing in the door's code before it was wrenched open and Dante's tall, muscular frame was taking up the doorway. I looked up at him and promptly burst into tears of relief and exhaustion.

"Holly, is Nate OK?" he asked in alarm.

"He's going to be fine," I said, nodding.

At that, he stepped forward and wrapped his arms around me. I clung at him, crying into the basketball shirt he was wearing. "Is that Holly?" I heard Jun from behind.

"Yeah," Dante confirmed, making no effort to move, other than to rub his hand over my back in large reassuring circles.

"Is she OK?"

I could feel Dante shrug under me. "I don't know."

Minhyuk appeared, squeezing through the small gap between Dante and the doorframe—the only member with a body skinny enough to ever consider accomplishing that. "She's soaking. Get her inside."

Obeying the younger member's instructions, Dante bent forward, scooping me up in his arms, and then carried me into the dorm. Without a word, we moved with purpose towards the room he and Minhyuk shared. Their bedding was already rolled out on the floor, and he gently deposited me in the middle of it.

When he stepped back, he finally caught sight of my face. "What the fuck?!" Dante exclaimed, his hand going for my cheek. His fingers brushed over the skin, and I couldn't stop the wince of pain as I jerked my head back.

Moments later, Minhyuk descended on me, wrapping me in towels. "What happened?" Behind him, Jun and Kyun appeared, moving into the room.

"What happened to your face?" Jun demanded, stepping forward beside Dante.

"She's shivering. Let her warm up first!" Kyun said, firmly.

Minhyuk paused: he had been towel drying my hair. "You're right. Holly, you're not going to get warm in wet clothes."

"I can help with that!" Jun offered, cheerfully. It earned him a smack upside the head from Dante.

"You need a shower," Minhyuk decided. Kyun disappeared from the room. Moments later, I heard the shower running.

I wasn't sure I would be able to stand up in one at this point, but he was right. I could not get warm. I got to my feet, with a little help from Dante, and then walked to the bathroom. Alone, I peeled the sodden dress from me, letting it fall with a splodge on the bathroom's tiled floor. My underwear was close behind. Then I stepped under the stream of water, hissing at its heat. I turned the temperature down a fraction, and then got in.

I stood under there for a very long time. My eyes

were fixed on my toes, and despite everything, my brain had switched off. I wasn't thinking about anything. I don't know how long I was in there for, but I eventually felt the heat return to my body. I got out, wrapping a fluffy towel around me.

When I stepped into the hallway to move to my room, I found all four guys waiting. "Go to bed," I sighed. "It must be nearly dawn."

"Your face," Minhyuk started.

I was aware of the throbbing, but I still hadn't looked in a mirror to see how bad it was. My fingers reached up to touch it, and I winced. There was definitely a bruise there. "Go to bed," I tried again.

"That's not going to happen, noona," Jun told me firmly, crossing his arms like he had the authority.

I was too tired to argue with one of them, much less four of them. "Fine," I grumbled. "Let me put some clothes on."

"No need on my account," Jun announced.

Dante once again smacked him upside the head.

I smiled, then moved into my bedroom, feeling like I had aged seventy years in the space of a few hours. I knew Jun meant well, but his flirting, the way the others were trying to look after me … all it did was make my stomach hurt.

I forced myself into some pajamas, and then I found the biggest hoodie I had and pulled that over the top, more for the comfort of something to hide in than the need for warmth. With my hood up, I stepped back into the hallway.

Dante, Minhyuk, Kyun, and Jun, were all still waiting. Wearily, I moved into the living room and settled onto one of the couches, bringing my feet up underneath me. I glanced out of the window. It was getting much lighter now.

A bowl of soup was thrust under my nose by Minhyuk. I gave it a sniff. "Is this haejangguk?" I asked suspiciously.

Minhyuk nodded. I pulled a face. Haejangguk was hangover soup and I was not hungover. "Haejangguk cures a hangover because it's predominately water, salt, and meat. It's everything your body craves." He looked me up and down. "It's what *your* body needs right now."

"Minhyuk makes great hangover soup," Jun told me.

"I haven't had a dish Minhyuk has made that wasn't great," I said, picking up the spoon and eating some. We were both right. So was Minhyuk. With each mouthful, I could feel myself feeling better and the last remnants of the chill disappeared from me. As I ate, Dante who was sitting on that side of me, held an icepack up to my face. It was a strange sensation, but it did help. So did not having to chew much. I finished the soup quickly.

"What happened?" Minhyuk asked, sitting in front of me on the floor. He leaned forward to take the bowl from me, setting it on the floor beside him.

I gave them the highlights, conveniently leaving out the conversation Nate and I had had outside the bathroom.

"Was it the girl?" Kyun asked, when I told them that Nate had been slipped a roofie. "The one who threw the eggs?"

I shrugged. "I don't know. I don't know if it was her. I don't know if it was someone who did it because they knew who he is. I don't know if it was just a complete coincidence," I said, becoming increasingly frustrated. I knew him being roofied wasn't my fault, but equally, if I hadn't told him about Kyun … No, if I had just kept things to Nate and myself—or even better, if I had just respected the fact I was his manager—then none of this would have happened. Nate wouldn't have gotten angry, and he wouldn't have been drinking as much.

I yawned. "What time is it?"

"About six," Dante replied. "You should get some sleep."

"You should all get some sleep," I said. "Tae is being discharged in a few hours. Nate should be soon after that."

Beside me, Jun frowned. "You need to sleep too."

I wasn't convinced I would sleep, even if I wanted to. Besides, I had other things to do. "Jun, I need to go to the police," I told him, getting to my feet.

"The police will want to get a statement from Nate," Kyun spoke up. He had been leaning against the wall, listening carefully to everything with a small frown on his face. "You may as well get a little bit of sleep and then go to them tomorrow with Nate."

Jun and Dante both reached up and pulled me back down. "Guys, I have a job to do." I frowned. "In fact, so do you. You all need to be somewhere for recording."

"The same recording you cancelled because Tae was being released?" Minhyuk asked, softly.

There was a feeling of déjà vu at that—like I'd had that conversation recently. "Did I?"

"And that right there is why you need some sleep," Dante pointed out.

Kyun folded his arms. "If you don't sleep, I won't."

With Tae in the hospital, I didn't doubt that. "I don't think I can sleep," I said. I also knew that I needed to break my promise because I didn't think the knot of guilt in my stomach would allow me to share a bed with him. Without realizing I was doing it, I clutched at my stomach and the sharp stabbing pain.

"Holly, are you OK?" Minhyuk asked, seeing it instantly.

"I don't think my body agrees with me eating this early," I mumbled dismissively. I was not about to tell them why that was hurting this morning.

"Movie time!" Jun declared, reaching for the television remote.

I was expecting someone to stop him, but surprisingly, no one did. I wasn't interested in watching a film, but it did mean that there would be no conversation for a while. Minhyuk had yet to stay awake during any movie we'd watched. If they'd been up all night, maybe they would fall asleep and I could leave for the office?

By mid-morning when it was time to leave to collect Tae and Nate from hospital, none of us had slept. I couldn't tell you what film we'd watched either. I felt like a zombie—most of my actions becoming automatic. The others had wanted to come too, but I had put my foot down, saying that if there was press there, it would be too much.

Tae was my first stop. He was looking remarkably cheerful at the prospect of leaving. He'd even managed to fix his hair and get a hint of makeup on him. In some respects, I was glad. There had been a small crowd of fans outside, and it would be good for them to see him looking so healthy. The driver had already left to take Tae's bags downstairs when Tae stopped me from leaving the room. I blinked up at him. I was so tired, he had a slight blur to his edges.

"Are you OK?" he asked me. He was staring at the bruise on my face in horror. I was surprised he hadn't said anything while the driver was in the room.

"It looks worse than it is," I admitted, wishing I had done something to cover it up, but the zombie which had taken over me hadn't even permitted me to think about that until we were at the hospital and a nurse was asking me if I was there to have it looked at. I sighed. "Tae, I have something to tell you."

"Me too," he declared, although he was still looking at my face dubiously. "I like you."

The stabbing pain reappeared in my side. Biting at my lip to try to mask my pain, my hand clutched at my hip. "Tae," I started.

"I know I told you that before, and I know that I then got mad when you didn't tell me who your father was," he said, cutting me off. "I'm sorry about that. I didn't handle it well, I know. But the truth is, while I've been in here, all I can think about is you. I've missed you." Taking care with his arm, he stepped forward, pulling me into an embrace.

"Tae," I said, starting to pull away.

Tae leaned down, kissing me.

My hands went up to his chest, and gently, I pushed him off me. "Nate is in the hospital," I blurted out.

Tae's eyes went wide, alarm settling in them. "Why?" he demanded. "What happened? Is he OK?"

"We're picking him up next," I said, pulling myself out of Tae's hold. "We went out last night—"

"Who?"

"Just me, him, and JongB," I said. I was starting to feel like a drone.

"Damnit!" Tae cried. "Has he been fighting again?" He stepped back and raked a hand through his hair. "I thought he'd managed to stop all that dumb shit." All of a sudden, he looked murderous. "Does this have anything do with your face?"

"Nate had his drink spiked!" I cried, holding my hands up.

"He wasn't fighting?" Tae repeated, surprised, yet relieved.

"Not exactly," I sighed. I rubbed at my face, then winced. Tae strode over, grasping my hands in his. "Outside of the club, some guy started hitting on me. Nate came to help, but he missed. I think it was because of the drugs, because he wouldn't have hit me intentionally."

Tae's anger ebbed. "He was protecting you?"

I nodded. "He was trying."

Tae pulled me back into his arms. "Then I am glad. I'll thank him when we see him. Is he OK?"

"The doctor told me he could come home this morning," I said, my words coming out mumbled against Tae's chest. I breathed him in, and the stabbing pain reappeared. Oh god, this guilt was going to kill me. "We need to go get him now."

제20 장

H3R오

Pain, The Love Of Heart

My stomach had been in agony from walking out of Tae's room, and progressively getting worse as we went to get Nate. I was fully aware this was nothing less than I deserved, but I was praying that Nate wouldn't say anything.

"Do you remember what happened?" Tae asked him.

Nate glanced at me, wincing at the bruise, then shook his head. "I don't remember much of last night," he added, giving me a pointed look.

Did that mean he didn't remember the fight, or everything leading up to it? With Tae not leaving our sides, I had no opportunity to ask him. In the end, we had bundled him up in the back of the minibus, where he had promptly fallen asleep, leaning against his leader.

I sat in the front, feeling like I was going to pass out the closer we got to the dorm. I had a bad feeling and I couldn't shake it.

Never had I made such an understatement.

Tae opened the door and stepped in. Before Nate could follow, Kyun has pushed Tae to the side and swung his fist at Nate, hitting him clean in the eye. Then things descended into chaos.

All rational thought just left me, and all I could do was stand there, screaming.

Dante jumped in, getting his arms under Kyun's shoulders and dragging him away from Nate before he could hit him again, Tae right behind him, yelling at him to calm down. Minhyuk went to Nate to make sure he was OK.

And then Jun was with me, pulling me outside, out of the way. "Stay here," he told me.

I shook my head. I knew why they were fighting, and this was definitely all my fault, I needed to try to fix it. I ducked past Jun and into the dorm. He followed me in, shutting the door behind us.

"Has it ever occurred to you that I should be the one punching you," Nate snapped at Kyun, rubbing at his jaw.

"She got hurt because you couldn't keep it in your pants!" Kyun yelled at him. Dante had let go of him, but he was very clearly standing with him to make sure he didn't go for Nate again. "Who is the girl?"

"What in god's name is going on here?" Tae demanded. Judging from the expressions on everyone's faces, he was the only one who didn't have a clue.

Kyun leaned down, grabbing an iPad which had been discarded on the couch beside them and practically shoved it Tae's face. Tae took it from him, scrolling through something.

"What is that?" I asked, now the confused one.

"It's all over the SNS and media," Minhyuk sighed, almost apologetically as Tae walked over to give me the iPad. I didn't miss the look he gave Nate as he passed him.

I took the device and felt my blood run cold. The first thing I saw was the image of me being punched by Nate. I started scrolling and the next picture was of Nate and the mystery woman all over each other in the club. That one hurt more than being punched in the face.

Nate turned, looking over my shoulder. "Who is she?"

"Who is she?" Kyun exploded. "You punched Holly!"

"It was an accident," I told him, calmly. "A guy grabbed me and Nate came to help. Unfortunately, because he was drugged, he hit me." I was surprised at how robotic I sounded. It was almost like I was listening to someone else speak.

"Is that who drugged me?" Nate asked.

"She looks familiar," Jun added, peering over. I looked at him, and his eyes went wide with recognition. "Yes! She isn't the girl who was throwing eggs at you, but she's been at all our appearances."

"Are you sure?" I asked, staring at the woman. I never paid much attention to the crowds, but it seemed odd that she would turn up at the club where we were.

"I would say Nate has a sasaeng."

Nate gave Tae a wary looked. "A *sasaeng*? Really?" A sasaeng was an extreme fan—the crazy ones that obsessed over an idol and pretty much stalked them. Although they were technically the opposite of an anti-fan, supposedly doing whatever they did because they loved their favorite idol so much, I personally classed them as the same thing. I certainly didn't like the idea of tagging the word 'fan' on there.

"She claims she's dating you, and has been for some time," Tae shrugged.

Could things possibly get any worse?

No sooner did that thought cross my mind, I regretted it.

They did.

"I'm not dating her, I'm dating Holly," Nate said, pulling a face. "The whole article is bullshit."

The room fell deathly silent and slowly, all eyes fell on Nate.

"Oh, this isn't good," I heard Jun mutter.

"You can't be dating her," Tae frowned. "She's with me."

"OK, how about we focus on this article and Nate's sasaeng?" Jun asked, brightly. The other five members ignored him, all turning to face me.

The knot in my stomach seemed to have been replaced with something equally as big, but this time it was spikey. "Holly, what's going on?" Kyun asked me, his expression dark.

I swallowed. Or I tried. There seemed to be some form of cactus in there. "I …" I tried.

"I don't think this is the important thing here," Jun said again. I wanted to hug him, but at the same time, I wanted to warn him to keep away. I also wanted to know why he was so eager to change the subject.

"It's not," Dante told him. "But that's because she isn't with you." There was something in Jun's expression which had Dante's eyebrows shooting into his hairline. "She is?"

"I can explain," I said, weakly. That was a lie—I had no idea where to start with any of this.

"Please do," said Tae, coldly.

This was it. This was the moment I had been dreading. "First of all, please don't turn on each other," I begged. "The one in the wrong is me. None of you knew what was happening with each other, so if you're going to hate someone, then that should be me. I deserve it." I could feel the tears building in the corner of my eyes, and I did my best to blink them away: I did deserve this. "I didn't set out to hurt anyone, and when I started to get myself back together and functioning, I realized I was falling in love with you all. I really didn't want to hurt anyone, but I didn't know how I could choose."

"Who says you have to?" Jun asked, quietly.

"What?" Dante asked. "Have to what?"

"Choose," Jun shrugged.

"At this point, I think that decision is made for me," I told him. "And I understand that."

Jun shook his head. "No, I mean, why should you have to choose?" he said again.

This time it was Nate's turn to sigh. "Jun, we've been over this. I don't see how this could work."

"How what could work?" Kyun demanded. "And what do you mean you've been over it. Did you two know?"

Despite everything that was happening, I couldn't stop my eyes going between Jun and Nate. I'd had a suspicion for a long time that Jun knew, even though he had continued to spend time with me. He'd kissed me—and more. But Nate too?

"I told Jun I had feelings for Holly," Nate admitted. "A while later he admitted the same, and that he thought you guys did too. I didn't believe it, especially not after me and Holly slept together."

"*You* slept with Holly?" Kyun cried in disbelief.

Minhyuk held his hands up as Dante put a warning hand on Kyun's arm. "I want to hear this out."

"You too?" Kyun asked. When Minhyuk nodded, Kyun shook his arm free of Dante's grip and stalked over to stand near the television, glowering at everyone as he folded his arms.

"What is there to hear out?" Tae asked. "Holly can't be with all of us. She needs to pick one."

My mouth fell open. Pick one? Tae still wanted something between us after all this? Even more astonishing was he thought I would be able to choose. That was part of what had put me in this mess to start with.

"Who says she has to, hyung?" Jun asked, carefully.

"Me, for one," Kyun snorted.

"Let's hear Jun out," Minhyuk insisted.

"There is no need to listen to any more nonsense from the maknae," Kyun said, shooting a look at the member in question.

"No, I want to hear this too," Dante said, quietly.

"It's not difficult," Jun shrugged. "We all like Holly. She likes all of us. Why make her choose? Why can't she be with all of us?"

"Unfortunately for you, maknae, there is no amount of money on this earth that will ever have you and I hooking up," Kyun told Jun, firmly.

Jun pulled a face. "That's not what I mean."

"She's with all of us, but not at the same time," Nate sighed, turning to Jun. "See, I told you that they would never go for it."

"Are you saying you'd be happy with that?"

Minhyuk asked Nate, tilting his head.

"I wasn't sure," Nate told him. "Last night, I almost decided on a flat-out no when Holly said she had slept with Kyun."

"What?" Tae demanded, glaring at me, then back at Kyun, who shot Tae a defiant scowl. I winced at the look he gave me, and bowed my head. This was a mess.

"And now?" Jun asked, trying again to help me out.

Nate looked at me, then back to Minhyuk, slowly nodding. "I'd at least want to try."

"I'm able to do it," Jun declared, folding his arms. "I've known the whole time. Makes no difference to me."

"You're an idiot," Kyun said, rolling his eyes.

"I would need to think about it," Minhyuk said, pursing his lips.

"This is bullshit!" Kyun snapped. "How can you even consider it. She picks one."

"What does Holly want?" Dante asked, looking at me. "No one has asked you that."

I blinked. Two minutes ago, I was certain I wouldn't ever be able to be with any of them, and now this? I didn't even know what to think. My brain couldn't handle the thought process fast enough and I was fairly certain my emotions had short-circuited at this point.

Before I could answer, there was an urgent knock on the door, which developed into a hammer. Jun opened it. Park Inhye was there looking completely frazzled. "Holly, why are you not answering your phone?"

I had to think about what she was asking me; the

question seemed so normal compared to everything else. "It died," I told her. It had died last night and it had never occurred to me to charge it. "Why?"

"We have a problem and you all need to pack right now!" she cried, bursting into the apartment.

"What's wrong?" I asked, alarmed, though thankful to have something else to focus on.

"Your brother is an asshole."

"And the sky is blue, but I'm not about to have a meltdown over the color of the sky," I pointed out, curious as to what Sejin had done this time.

"I was going through the emails—there's another account that had been created that you hadn't been given access to—and I found one for a sponsorship deal with a hotel on Jeju Island."

"That's a bad thing?" I asked, thinking the opposite.

Inhye shook her head. "The sponsorship part is a brilliant opportunity for H3RO. The problem is that Sejin signed it. They're expecting you today for the next ten days for a photoshoot and some video commercials."

"Then we need to rearrange it," I said. "We have a schedule."

"If you cancel or rearrange it then you—H3RO, not Atlantis—are going to get sued. You've only just made enough money for the legal fees. This will destroy H3RO," she told me. Then she pulled something out of her purse and thrust it at me: passports and tickets. "I'm working through rescheduling what you have in Seoul this week, and seeing if anything can be moved to Jeju, but you've got three hours to get to the airport to get on the flight out there, so you need to move quickly. I'll take care of as much of it as I can from here, but you need to go, Holly. Now."

"OK," Tae agreed for me. He looked around the room. "We'll finish our discussion later when we get to Jeju. Right now, we have cases to pack and a flight to catch."

Just like that, H3RO listened to their leader, running off to their rooms. I watched them go while Inhye handed over a stack of information, including the contract. Then she disappeared so I could get ready, promising there would be two minibuses downstairs waiting for us in no more than ten minutes.

I watched her leave, then stared down at the pile of papers in my hands. It felt like everything was imploding in on me and yet the only thing I could think about was Jun's words: *Why can't she be with all of us?*

No, there would be time to think of that later.

There would be a very awkward and uncomfortable hour-long flight to think about this.

Right now, I had to make sure H3RO got on that flight, before Sejin got his way and H3RO didn't exist anymore.

Then I would see if they could survive me.

To be continued …

… H3RO's story is not over yet!

If you've enjoyed what you've read so far, please, please leave a quick review on Amazon! They really help authors out and I (like H3Ro) would appreciate all the help we given.

Sign up to Ji Soo's newsletter to receive release alerts, and keep tabs on the other groups at Atlantis Entertainment (did you know Bright Boys had recently debuted?):

Head to
https://sendfox.com/JSLee
to sign up

CHAPTER TITLES

The chapters in this book are all named after song titles:

1. *Tell Them* by Block B
2. *DNA* by BTS
3. *Hot Boy* by Bigstar
4. *Seoul Night* by Teen Top
5. *Take A Shot* by Hotshot
6. *Road to Stardom* by Bigflo
7. *Stop Stop It* by Got7
8. *Power* by EXO
9. *Don't Touch My Girl* by Boyfriend
10. *Sorry For My English* by In2it
11. *Going Crazy* by UP10TION
12. *Calling You* by Highlight
13. *Runaway* by Pentagon
14. *While You Were Sleeping* by HALO
15. *Way Back Home* by BTOB
16. *Just That Little Thing* by MYNAME
17. *Boom Boom* by Seventeen
18. *Black Out* by N-Sonic
19. *Nightmare* by Romeo
20. *Pain, The Love of Heart* by SPEED

CHARACTER BIOGRAPHIES

H3RO

Name: H3RO (헤로)
Fandom: Treasure
Colors: Purple
Debut: 2012-03-15

H3RO consists of 6 members:
Tae, Dante, Nate, Minhyuk, Kyun and Jun.

The group debuted on March 15th, 2012.

Stage Name: Tae (태)

Birth Name: Park Hyun-Tae (박현태)
Position: Leader, Vocalist
Birthday: March 1st
Age: 27
Zodiac sign: Pisces
Height: 182 cm

Weight: 62 kg
Blood Type: A

Tae facts:
He was born in: Incheon, South Korea
Family: Mother
If H3RO were a family, he would be the dad
Takes the role of leader very seriously
Protective of his group
Has a short temper
He shares a room with Kyun
Speaks Korean and Japanese

Stage Name: Dante (단테)

Birth Name: Guan Feng (关峰 / 풍관)
Position: Main vocals, visual
Birthday: June 24th
Age: 25
Zodiac sign: Cancer
Height: 183 cm
Weight: 72 kg
Blood Type: O

Dante facts:
He was born in: Hong Kong, Hong Kong
Family: father, mother
If H3RO were a family, he would be the rebellious son

The member who spends the most time in front of the mirror
He shares a room with Minhyuk
His favorite food is chicken
Speaks Chinese, Korean, and English
Sleeps naked

Stage Name: Minhyuk (민혁)

Birth Name: Kwon Min-Hyuk (권민혁)

Position: Rapper (high), dancer
Birthday: May 24th
Age: 24
Zodiac sign: Gemini
Height: 176 cm
Weight: 60 kg
Blood Type:

Minhyuk facts:
He was born in: Ulsan, South Korea
Family: father, mother
If H3RO were a family, he would be the mom
Loves cleaning
He shares a room with Dante
The mood maker of the group
Speaks Korean and Japanese

Stage Name: Nate (네이트)
Birth Name: Nathan Choi
Position: Dancer, rapper (low)
Birthday: May 11ᵗʰ
Age: 24
Zodiac sign: Taurus
Height: 178 cm
Weight: 58 kg
Blood Type: AB

Nate facts:
He was born in: San Francisco, USA
Family: father, mother
He shares a room with Jun
The peacemaker of the group
His favorite food is sushi
Speaks English and Korean
Is no good at chat-up lines

Stage Name: Kyun (균)
Birth Name: Ha Kyun-Gu (하균구)
Position: Vocals

Birthday: February 3rd
Age: 23
Zodiac sign: Aquarius
Height: 181 cm
Weight: 65 kg
Blood Type: B

Kyun facts:
He was born in: Incheon, South Korea
Family: Doesn't speak about them
He shares a room with Tae
Often reacts to uncomfortable situations with anger
Does not eat meat, but will eat fish
His favorite food is ramen

Stage Name: Jun (준)

Birth Name: Song Jun-Ki (송준기)
Position: Maknae, vocals
Birthday: February 18th
Age: 23
Zodiac sign: Aquarius
Height: 175 cm
Weight: 65 kg
Blood Type: AB

Jun facts:
He was born in Hwaseong, South Korea
Family: Father, mother

He shares a room with Nate
Enjoys photography
Hardest member to wake up
Can fall asleep anywhere
Pizza
Previously known as JunK

ACKNOWLEDGEMENTS

First and foremost, I need to thank you—you who is reading this. If you're reading this, it means you liked Idol Thoughts enough to want to keep reading. That alone fills me with so much gratitude I could hug all of you. I hope you fell in love with H3RO as much as I did! I'd ask who your favorite was, but then I'd have to make you choose, and the whole point is, why should you?

As always, love and gratitude goes to my publisher and friend, Cheryl. Sometimes, we're so on the "same page" (as Cheryl likes to say), that we could be sharing the same brain. Thank you for keeping me going, and for getting me started! Cheryl is also the one responsible for introducing me to two of the best people I know: Sarah and Leanne. Together we have rounded out characters and gotten distracted by the likes of 24K, iKON and Monsta X. I regret nothing. One day, I hope we can meet and fangirl in person. Until then, I will just send you love and gratitude in the shape of pictures of Bobby and B.I.

Once more I have a truly beautiful cover from Natasha at Natasha Snow Designs. It's so pretty, I think I'm going to print it out and frame it! When I couldn't offer much more than, "This is BTS. Can you somehow turn the K-Pop video into a cover for a Reverse Harem?" you blew me away with capturing that for me. Thank you for my work of art! Also, welcome to the ARMY.

Once again my beta readers and ARC readers, who I feel really should be called Life Savers, have all my gratitude and appreciation. Seriously, you guys read fast, and you can still pick out those pesky typos. You are truly awesome! Thank you so very much! Megan, Vanessa, Courtney, Melinda, Heather, Jessica, Karmen, Janie and Adena– you really are the greatest!

ATLANTIS ENTERTAINMENT NEWSLETTER

Would you like to be kept up to date on the antics of the idols and artists at Atlantis Entertainment? Sign up to the Atlantis Entertainment Newsletter, managed by the silent Chairwoman of Atlantis Entertainment, Ji Soo.

Ji Soo will keep you updated on the Atlantis Roster, as well as providing you with a healthy dose of K-Pop, some Korean culture, and if she can persuade her 할머니 (that's Korean for 'grandmother', pronounced halmeoni) to part with some cherished recipes, some of those, along with some reading recommendations. There may even be a few insights into her crazy life. But probably not, because her life is very boring …

Find out more at:

https://sendfox.com/JSLee

ABOUT THE AUTHOR

Ji Soo Lee is the Korean name of this Texan-born Korean-American author. She spends most of her days lost in a K-Pop haze, which inspired her to start writing stories about her idols at Atlantis Entertainment.

Under the name Ji Soo Lee, you will find YA contemporary romances, with romance levels like a K-Drama.

Under J. S. Lee, Ji Soo writes steamier stories, mainly of Reverse Harems

WAYS TO CONNECT

Facebook
Author Page:
https://www.facebook.com/OfficialJiSooLee
Atlantis Fan Group:
https://www.facebook.com/groups/AtlantisEnts/

Bookbub:
https://www.bookbub.com/authors/j-s-lee

Amazon:
https://www.amazon.com/J.-S.-Lee/e/B07H353S3L

Instagram:
https://www.instagram.com/ji_soo_lee_author/

Website:
www.jisooleeauthor.com

Made in the USA
Las Vegas, NV
14 March 2021